How the Lady Seduce

How the Lady Seduced the Viscount

Laura A. Barnes

Laura A. Barnes

2021

First Printing: 2021

ISBN: 9798494859938

Laura A. Barnes

Website: www.lauraabarnes.com

Cover Art by Cheeky Covers

Editor: Telltail Editing

To: William

Thank you for your unwavering support and encouragement. Also for your patience when I don't always pay attention, because I'm lost in my stories. I promise one day I won't make you keep repeating yourself. I love you!

Cast of Characters

Hero ~ Griffen Kincaid

Heroine ~ Jacqueline Holbrooke

Uncle Theo ~ Duke of Colebourne

Lucas Gray ~ Colebourne's son

Susanna Forrester ~ Colebourne's sister-in-law

Ramsay Forrester ~ Lady Forrester's husband

Charlotte Holbrooke ~ Colebourne's niece

Jasper Sinclair ~ Charlotte's husband

Evelyn Holbrooke ~ Colebourne's niece

Reese Worthington ~ Evelyn's husband

Gemma Holbrooke ~ Colebourne's niece

Barrett Ralston ~ Gemma's husband

Abigail Cason ~ Colebourne's ward

Lady Worthington ~ Reese's mother

Graham (Worth) Worthington ~ Reese's brother

Eden Worthington ~ Reese's sister

Noel Worthington ~ Reese's sister

Lord Falcone ~ Colebourne's guest

Chapter One

Griffen Kincaid leaned his arm on the windowsill and stared out at the rainy landscape. He had spent the last four days of his visit at the Colebourne estate trapped indoors, waiting for a break in the stormy weather. At least the bride and groom had made their escape before the storms hit.

He had remained as a guest after the wedding ceremony with promises of fishing and hunting. The duke had also agreed to discuss his investment in a business venture Kincaid hoped to pursue. If he secured the deal, then it would loosen the control the duke kept him under. During his younger years as he sowed his wild oats, he'd involved himself in a scandal, one the duke had helped him to escape from but also trapped Kincaid into jumping to the duke's command whenever Colebourne snapped his fingers.

The trip from London hadn't held much promise. He'd agreed to stand up with his best mate, Lucas Gray, while he married Lady Selina Pemberton, who Gray had been engaged to for his entire life. In the end, he'd spoken no marital vows to her. No. Gray's cousin Duncan Forrester had won the privilege with his declaration of love. With any other family, the destruction would have had insurmountable repercussions, but this family had accepted the change of grooms with nothing but pure happiness for the newly wedded couple. Gray's other family members held the same eccentric traits as the old man.

No. The correct definition of the Colebourne family was mad. Pure madness.

And Kincaid feared he held the same madness as the rest of them. All because of his attraction to one Jacqueline Holbrooke. A lady he'd carried on an affair with over the past three years, against his better judgement. A lady who, at every opportunity, refused his offers of marriage. He couldn't walk away from her either. Not for the reason of his scandalous behavior he entangled himself in as a gentleman with an innocent lady, but because his body refused to deny itself the pleasure he found in her arms, not to mention the love he held in his heart for her. He played with fire, but he no longer cared.

Before he made his departure from Colebourne Manor, he would have secured himself a bride. Kincaid would no longer accept her refusal.

~~~~~

Jacqueline Holbrooke sat in the corner of the drawing room with the other ladies, pretending to sew. However, her gaze kept straying to Lord Kincaid. The handsome lord stared out the window, brooding. His misery at being trapped indoors while the rain kept falling was more than evident.

A secretive smile spread across her face. She wondered if she could entice him to sneak away for a few stolen moments, or perhaps even longer. She yearned for his kisses and the caress of his sensuous touch. Jacqueline had missed their stolen moments greatly over the past few nights. At first, they hadn't been able to sneak into each other's bedchambers because Uncle Theo had placed a servant in the secret passageway to keep Duncan and Selina apart. Then Kincaid had refused the invitations to visit her bedchamber and had yet to explain his reasons. Instead, he stayed awake into the early morning hours, playing billiards, smoking cigars, and drinking
~~~~~

with the other gentlemen. One would think he avoided Jacqueline on purpose.

However, at every opportunity when they found themselves alone, Kincaid teased her with his kisses. He pulled her into secret alcoves, dark closets, or abandoned rooms. Each kiss built her need to be held in his arms for hours of lovemaking. After he stroked her desire, he would saunter away with a wicked grin, leaving Jacqueline trembling for their next tryst.

When she first allowed Kincaid such liberties, she'd thought the passion would burn itself out. Instead, it only stretched further out of her reach. While the rational part of her argued to halt her encounters with the viscount, the emotional part of her hungered for his uncontrollable appetite. She needed to stop this obsession before her uncle caught wind of their affair. With his mad matchmaking schemes, he would insist upon a union.

Jacqueline had no intention of getting married.

No, she enjoyed her independence too much to find herself shackled to her husband's every demand. With only her and Abigail left, Jacqueline must remain vigilant.

She knew she was next judging by the whispers and Aunt Susanna's constant attention. The only advantage she held was her knowledge of how they played their matchmaking games and her wisdom on how to avoid them. She'd watched how they'd manipulated their other victims over the past few months. Or, in Charlie's case, how they'd made her part of a bet. The victor had won Charlie's hand in marriage, which had forced Evelyn into a marriage filled with lies, leading her to endure a rocky start until love overcame their deceit. Gemma's marriage to Ralston and Duncan's recent wedding to Selina were forbidden love matches. Uncle Theo and Aunt Susanna dangled the forbiddance of their relationship, tempting the couples into secrecy.

Duncan and Selina's match came to be because of her cousin Lucas and his affection for Abigail Cason. Abigail was a ward her uncle had adopted when Jacqueline, her sisters, and their cousin Gemma moved in with him. Abigail was like a sister to them. The feelings Abigail and held Lucas for each other were fragile and had become more vulnerable when Lucas's marriage to Selina drew closer.

Jacqueline couldn't even claim Uncle Theo and Aunt Susanna had manipulated Duncan into marrying Selina because the love they held for one another was more than obvious. In time, the brother and sister-in-law would conjure their matchmaking spell on Lucas and Abigail.

For now, Jacqueline would become their next victim. She must stay on guard and keep one step ahead of them.

"Jacqueline, Lord Kincaid appears out of sorts with the endless rain. Perhaps you should see if he would like for you to read to him." Aunt Susanna's voice rang out for the entire room to hear.

A blush spread across Jacqueline's cheeks at her aunt's obvious display of matchmaking.

Lord Kincaid stiffened and slowly turned in their direction. His gaze narrowed on them. "I am more than capable of reading a book, Lady Forrester."

Aunt Susanna released a silly giggle, and Jacqueline narrowed her gaze at her aunt's girlish behavior. "Of course you are, Lord Kincaid. You only appear bored beyond tears, and our Jacqueline has such a lovely voice."

Lord Kincaid centered his gaze on Jacqueline. Its intensity caused Jacqueline to squirm in the chair. He blatantly declared his interest with his stare. "Yes, she does. On that, I will agree, Lady Forrester."

Kincaid watched the blush spread along Jacqueline's neck at his compliment. It was refreshing to know that even after all their assignations, she still held a bit of innocence and hadn't become too jaded for him to charm.

"Well, then off with you two. The library should be less full than this overcrowded room." Lady Forrester raised her hand, implying for them to follow her orders.

Kincaid nodded. The lady may have appeared silly, but Lady Forrester was nothing if not shrewd. He watched her, along with Colebourne, manipulate each couple in this room into a union. He would use their interference to his advantage. If Colebourne approved of him as an adequate suitor for Jacqueline, then she would have no choice but to accept his proposal.

He held out his hand to help Jacqueline from her chair. "Shall we, my lady?"

Jacqueline's hand trembled in his, and he held back a smile of victory. The knowledge of how his touch affected her pleased him. He had remained absent from her bed the past week to entice her to accept his marriage proposal. With each kiss he stole, he left her craving more. However, when he teased her, he tormented himself instead. He decided not to pressure her any longer. He would bide his time until the right moment came upon them, then pledge his undying devotion to her. For now, he would enjoy Colebourne and Lady Forrester throwing him in front of Jacqueline's path.

Jacqueline bowed her head demurely, allowing him to draw her out of the drawing room and into the hallway. What was the minx up to now? Before he could wonder, she yanked her hand from him and stalked away. What had caused a rise in her dander? He followed in amusement, watching her hips sway back and forth. She made for quite a sight in her agitation. Especially when she turned and glared at him as they reached the library. Her breasts heaved with each drawn breath. The heavenly globes pushed against the trim of her gown, and his gaze stay focused on them for too long. His only excuse was that he forgot himself, hungering for a taste of her creamy skin.

"Lord Kincaid?" Jacqueline growled.

He raised his gaze in amusement to find Jacqueline regarding him with barely contained fury. "Yes, my love."

Jacqueline scanned the library to make sure they were alone. "Do not address me as such. I am not your love."

Kincaid couldn't help himself. He needed to touch her. He slid his finger along her cheek and whispered in her ear, "I beg to differ. Why else do I warm your bed upon each of my visits?"

Jacqueline shivered from his touch. Her body screamed for him to kiss her. However, she was upset that he'd fallen for Aunt Susanna's matchmaking attempt. She must warn him of her family's schemes. Even though the scoundrel before her kept proposing, she refused to fall victim to Uncle Theo's manipulations.

She swiped his hand away. "You share my bed to scratch an itch, Lord Kincaid, and for no other reason alone. I am well aware of your exploits outside of my bedchamber."

He chuckled his amusement. "They are false."

Jacqueline pinched her lips. "That is not what they whisper in the crowded ballrooms."

"Complete falsehoods. I assure you, my lady, I have not visited another lady's bed since we became involved."

Jacqueline twitched slightly before she turned to stalk away from him. She needed to put some much-needed distance between them. His very nearness rattled her senses. “It does not matter to me in the slightest.”

“Mmm. So you declare, but your reaction states otherwise.” Kincaid slid his arm around Jacqueline’s waist and drew her against him.

Jacqueline trembled when his lips brushed across the back of her neck. She closed her eyes, dropping her head back against his chest. His hand traveled higher, brushing across her breasts. Her nipples tightened from the brief caress. She must issue her warning, but her body begged for her silence while she captured his attention.

His lips trailed to her ear, and he whispered, “Do you notice how your body trembles in my embrace?” Kincaid’s fingers dipped inside her bodice, teasing the valley of her breasts. “How your nipples have tightened into firm buds, begging for my tongue?”

He continued to torment Jacqueline with his gentle touch, teasing her to the verge of denial. Each kiss and stroke of his fingers drew her closer to succumbing to their desire. His own resistance stood near the edge of crumbling with each moan she drew forth.

“Griffen,” Jacqueline moaned.

He trailed his lips along her cheek to the corner of her lips. “And if I were to lift your skirts and slide my hand between your thighs, would I find you wet for me?” His tongue traced her lips. “Do you still wish to claim my pursuits do not matter to you?”

Griffen had worked Jacqueline into a frenzy. A declaration of her feelings almost escaped from her lips. She would confess her deepest secrets as long as he never denied her the exquisite pleasure of his touch. She ached for the brush of his lips against hers.

Jacqueline turned her head for their lips to connect, but he pulled back. Her eyes flew open to see his devious smile. Then he dropped his hands and sauntered away, leaving her frazzled.

He needed to calm his libido before he took her against the bookcases. At his first touch, she'd melted in his arms, her body begging him to make love to her. Hell, his own body begged him to take her into his arms again and finish what he'd started. He might have intended to tease her, but it'd backfired against him, only making him crave her more than ever.

Griffen's head swiveled toward the window. Damn this rain. It only trapped him closer to her.

Griffen turned back toward Jacqueline when the silence continued. Their gazes met and held. Each expected the other to confess their affections. He refused to budge on his stand, and she refused to accept his proposal, which left the passion drawing them toward each other to control their actions of denial. And like always, he would concede because he was powerless to deny her.

He held out a hand. "Jacqueline?"

She shook her head at him, wrapping her arms around her waist. She knew he regretted teasing her with his whispered words. Jacqueline was as much at fault. Her body responded, showing him her most inner desires. Every whispered word spoke the truth. Even now, she hungered for him to continue. She now understood his game. He wanted a commitment and withheld his affections. She couldn't blame him. She led him on each time she invited him to her bed.

Many would call her a fool for resisting him as a husband. He was quite the catch. Tall, handsome, witty, smart, and well-liked by all. Not to mention a tremendously generous lover. Oh, why she denied herself a lifetime of sharing his bed stumped even her. Especially when he lit her on fire and stroked her flames. As she stared at him, her body urged her to clasp his hand and follow him wherever he would lead them. Hopefully to his bedchamber or hers.

"Lord Kincaid, I must warn you not to fall victim to my uncle's scheme."

He dropped his hand once he realized she refused to take it. "And what scheme might that be, *Lady Jacqueline*?" If she wanted to act formally, then he would do so as well.

"The one where we end up as bride and groom."

Griffen shrugged. "Now why would I not want to fall victim to your uncle's matchmaking when it is the very outcome I desire? My multiple marriage proposals state my intentions. Your uncle's approval only helps my cause."

Jacqueline gritted her teeth. "It is not what I desire."

"Why not?"

"I do not have to explain myself."

Kincaid smirked. "No, you do not. Perhaps I will assist your uncle in his matchmaking scheme. Make it simple for him since it is not necessary for him to perform the same devious acts against us that he used on your sisters and cousins. Especially after I have already enjoyed your sensuous body on multiple occasions. Why deny what the outcome of our union will become? You will be mine."

His confident declaration annoyed Jacqueline. While he never showed this arrogant side of his character often, it held a sense of foreboding. Would he inform Uncle Theo of their affair? Or was it only a threat for her to succumb to his wishes? Either way, she needed to keep her defenses up. But if she guarded herself against his attention, then she denied herself the pleasure of the passion he ignited with his very presence.

"You would not dare," Jacqueline hissed.

His devious smile returned, and he arched a brow. "I would."

Jacqueline didn't answer him and stormed out of the library. He chuckled at her fury. She was usually an amiable lady with a level head. However, he flustered her into a vulnerable soul. She fought her emotions so as not to experience the pain of loss again. When he ignited her temper, Jacqueline's spirit came alive.

A spirit he hoped she never kept banked again.

Chapter Two

Kincaid sat between Jacqueline and Lady Eden Worthington at dinner that evening. It would appear the Duke of Colebourne and Lady Forrester still aimed to play matchmaker between him and Jacqueline. The entire situation held much irony because he would have rebuffed these attempts before his involvement with Jacqueline. Now he only found humor in them.

However, the lady held much dislike over her family's interference. At his every attempt to draw her into a conversation, she refused to utter a word in his direction, which left him to converse with Lady Eden for much of the meal. Not that it was a chore with this Worthington sister anyhow. Lady Eden was an intelligent conversationalist who was knowledgeable on many topics of interest.

This evening they discussed the bookshops of London. She had just finished her first season and had fallen in love with the many opportunities to broaden her educational horizon. He informed her of a few hidden bookstores for when she visited London again. When he told her he would leave word at them for her entry, Lady Eden thanked him before she turned her attention to her brother Graham.

At least Kincaid didn't have to endure the dinner with her sister, Lady Noel, at his side. The lady was quite charming, but she was on the hunt for a husband. Her glances toward him since they had arrived for Gray's wedding made Kincaid quite uncomfortable. At one time, her attention would have boosted his ego, but his heart remained true to the ravishing beauty at his side, the golden-haired temptress who smelled sinfully delicious. Her fragrance teased him throughout dinner, and he knew she wore the perfume he'd gifted her on purpose. The musky scent hovered between them, drawing on their desires. She meant to show her frustrations by teasing him. However, he only found satisfaction at riling her senses.

Jacqueline stewed in her seat. The seating arrangement only proved the point she attempted to convince Kincaid, a point he only brushed aside because it went along with his foolish agenda. What possessed him to continue with his chase? Why couldn't he just enjoy their secret rendezvouses? Was it because he needed financial security? That must be the reason for his pursuit.

She'd heard the rumors of his demise whispered in the ballrooms. How he'd barely scraped two coins together by selling off his properties that weren't entailed, and how he'd mortgaged the properties that were entailed to the hilt. He'd even rented his London townhome this season to an American family for a hefty amount of coin. Jacqueline would have been blind not to have noticed the state of his clothing since his return. While they were in fair condition, they were not of the current style. She wondered why he had fallen on hard times. Kincaid's demise hadn't escaped Uncle Theo's notice. However, her uncle must have seen potential in the viscount for him to approve of Kincaid as a suitor for Jacqueline. Her situation had taken a turn, and she realized the hopelessness of keeping her independence.

Kincaid was one of Lucas's oldest pals from his university days and had visited Colebourne Manor on many occasions. However, a few years had passed without him visiting. When he reappeared three years ago, he'd struck Jacqueline speechless. Those missing years had been very kind to him. No. Kind was too tame of a word to declare how he had transformed.

Once a tall gangly boy graced the halls, but on his return, a devastating god strolled through and dominated her senses. Even now, she trembled from his mere presence. He was tall with a thick wavy blond tame of hair pulled into a queue. Every time she stared into his turquoise eyes, they made her feel as if she floated in an ocean.

She took a peek out of the corner of her eye at his muscular form. She didn't know how he kept himself so firm, nor did she care. Her fingers curled into fists, fighting against her temptations. She ached to scrape her nails along his muscular thighs. She knew every delicious inch of him firsthand. His worn clothing did him no justice. However, the cut of his garments made him a striking figure indeed. The longer dinner continued, the more difficult she found resisting him.

"Lord Kincaid, I hope the weather has not swayed you to leave early?" Colebourne boomed from the end of the table.

"On the contrary, it has only heightened the pleasure of my visit," Kincaid replied.

Colebourne arched a brow. "Oh, how so?"

Kincaid relaxed back in his chair, his fingers brushing across Jacqueline's hand. "Why, it has given me a chance to become better acquainted with your charming niece, Lady Jacqueline."

Jacqueline bit back a gasp at his audacity. "Why, Lord Kincaid, you flatter me so." She tried to pull her hand away, but he kept it clasped firmly with his.

"Excellent. Perhaps tomorrow we can discuss the proposal we spoke of while in town. I am sure we can persuade each other to applicable terms," Colebourne said.

Kincaid nodded. "I think we can come to a beneficial agreement for all parties involved. I am at your disposal."

Colebourne sliced into his meal. "Then after breakfast it is." He took a bite before addressing the rest of the table. "Also, I am expecting a few more guests. We shall have a fox hunt and a formal dinner on Saturday to end this wedding celebration. Hopefully, the weather will break tomorrow for some outside activities. If not, then I am sure Lady Forrester has planned a few inside entertainments to keep us occupied."

"I am already ahead of you, Colebourne," Lady Forrester answered.

The table laughed at her readiness. While most of them were family, a few guests had lingered after the wedding. Kincaid tried to keep a hold of Jacqueline's hand, but she tore it away. Then she turned once again to speak with her sister's husband, Lord Sinclair. Their easygoing conversation and close friendship unnerved Kincaid, causing jealousy to course through him. He wanted to be the only gentleman she held an attachment to. When Jacqueline released a twinkling laugh, he snarled his annoyance.

"Is something the matter with your pheasant, Lord Kincaid?" Lady Forrester asked.

Kincaid covered his snarl with a charming smile. "No, 'tis most delicious. I remembered a matter I had forgotten to address before I left town."

Gray joined in. "I hope it is nothing too pressing."

Kincaid shook his head. "Nothing I cannot deal with from here. A simple letter sent tomorrow will sort out the issue."

Gray nodded. "That is swell. Another round of cards this evening?" he addressed the gentlemen around the table.

The single gentlemen agreed while the married ones pleaded their excuses once their wives frowned their disapprovals. Oh, how Kincaid envied them. Hopefully, before long, he would become one of those lucky gentlemen. Perhaps even as early as tomorrow, once he had his meeting with Colebourne. He would discuss his proposal with the duke, then offer for Jacqueline's hand.

While the rain had been a hindrance, his visit looked to improve remarkably. With a bit of luck, it might end with winning the lady who held his heart in the palm of her hand. Even as much as she resisted their connection, he felt confident she wanted the same future as he did. He only needed to prove she could keep her independence while still loving him. And if she allowed her walls to fall, she would realize he wasn't leaving, and loving someone helped to ease the ache she suffered from at the loss of her parents.

Jacqueline tried to keep up the pretense of showing interest in her conversation with Sinclair but failed greatly. She needed to stop Griffen from discussing their relationship with her uncle. If he mentioned his interest in becoming her husband, it would be the end of her comfortable existence of freedom. His firm hold of her hand spoke of his obvious intentions. He meant to ask Uncle Theo for her hand in marriage. Perhaps if she visited his bedchamber this evening, she could persuade him to change his mind. She would play on her fears of a committed relationship and convince him to give her a bit longer before she promised herself to him. This would buy her more time before he returned to London. Yes. That was what she would do. After he finished his gentlemen's pastime for the evening, she would tempt him with a more pleasurable pursuit.

"Jacqueline, does something trouble you this evening?" Sinclair asked.

She cleared her throat. "No. Why do you ask?"

"You appear quite distracted."

She attempted a laugh. "What nonsense you speak."

He quirked a brow. "Do I? You forget we have held a friendship for many years. I know when you are distressed. It is the same expression you hold whenever your sisters have troubled you."

Jacqueline sighed. "'Tis nothing I cannot handle."

"And when you cannot, will you at least unburden yourself? If not with my ear, then with your sisters."

Jacqueline smiled. "I promise I will."

Sinclair nodded before resuming his meal. She must be more careful. She seemed to wear her heart on her sleeve. If Sinclair noticed her distress, then it would only be a matter of time before her sisters became aware, too. She never could lie to them. If they discovered her involvement with Kincaid, they would urge her into a marriage with him. Since they were settled, they wanted Jacqueline to experience the same happiness, and with a promising candidate for a groom, they would become as relentless as Uncle Theo and Aunt Susanna. No amount of guilt would make her say I do. Not even the knowledge of her discarded virtue would make her marry.

No. Lord Kincaid needed to be handled, and handle him she would later this evening.

~~~~~

Jacqueline paced back and forth across her bedroom. She stopped for the umpteenth time by the mirror. Should she make another attempt at confronting Griffen? She had already gone to his bedchamber twice now. And both times, he still hadn't returned from the game room. However, the house had grown quiet, and it was way past the hour where the gentleman would continue to play cards. Why hadn't he returned?

She tightened the belt on her robe. Jacqueline didn't want to attract any unwanted attention, so she wore her most unflattering nightwear. She
~~~~~

wanted to keep Griffen focused on the reason for her visit. And it was to convince him not to speak with Uncle Theo of any marital intentions. Her visit to his bedchamber was for no other purpose.

She decided on one more attempt and opened the secret door, peeking out into the passageway. It stood empty. With hurried strides, she proceeded to his room, her steps leading the way on their own accord. Jacqueline didn't even need to count the doors, for her heart knew the direction of the other half of her soul.

What nonsense. Griffen was only a distraction. 'Twas nothing more.

The latch slipped undone for the third, and hopefully last, time this evening. When Jacqueline pushed the door open, the same greeting met her as before. A dark, empty chamber. She stormed inside and glared at the bed with her hands on her hips. He should bloody well be asleep by now. The longer she stared at the bed, the more her irritation seeped away, only to be replaced by a longing for what she had missed over the past week.

She reached out to trail her hand across the quilt, sinking her fingers into the softness. The bed beckoned her to crawl between the sheets to wait for Griffen, to lay her head upon his pillow and breathe in his masculine scent. Jacqueline took a step back from the temptation, but memories of them intertwined in the sheets caused her to halt.

Griffen's hard body rose above her, slowly stroking in and out of her. Their hands created a fiery sensation with each caress while their lips consumed each other with a passion known only to them. He would whisper the most romantic sentiments in her ear while making them one. Then his whispers would turn most scandalous as his mouth roamed over her body, drawing out her desires with each searing torch of his kiss.

Her body trembled to hear those whispered promises. Jacqueline's hand rose to her throat and slowly slid down until it rested on the belt of her robe. Her eyes drifted closed as she imagined Griffen loosening it while teasing her with light kisses. Her body grew warm at the memories awakening inside her.

A log on the fire shifted and sent out a hiss. She flinched at the noise and searched the room, afraid someone had caught her fantasizing in a bachelor's bedchamber. Once she realized it was only the fire, she calmed. There was no need for a servant to enter since the fire had already been lit. Griffen traveled with no valet. He had assured her the first evening they spent in his bedchamber that he had traveled alone on this visit.

She closed her eyes, gathering her thoughts. After she reminded herself of the reasons for her visit, Jacqueline decided she would wait for him. She settled on an oversized chair in front of the fire, curled her legs up underneath her, and laid her head on top of her knees. Her stare focused on the door as she waited for Griffen's return. It didn't take long before her eyes grew heavy, and she slid them closed. She would only rest for a few minutes...

However, Jacqueline fell asleep and missed her chance at confronting her dashing suitor when he strolled in.

~~~~~

Kincaid staggered to his bedchamber. He had overindulged again this evening while playing cards with Graham Worthington and Gray. The other gentlemen had called it an early evening, leaving the three bachelors to their own demise. However, it had ended very promisingly for Kincaid. He had won enough blunt off the card games to cover his living expenses for the next month in the boarding room he rented in London.

He threw open his door, and it slammed against the wall. Kincaid cringed at the booming noise. He glanced over his shoulder and breathed a
~~~~~

sigh of relief that he hadn't awoken a soul. At least he hoped he hadn't. If not, he would surely hear the complaint tomorrow morning at breakfast.

He shrugged off the disapproval that might greet him, which only proved how ripped his condition was. He closed the door much quieter and leaned against it, staring with longing toward the bed. As exhausted as he was, the emptiness still troubled him. A certain frustrating lady should have been lying in his bed, waiting for him without a stitch of clothing on. Mmm. Perhaps he should slip through the secret passageway and pay her a visit. The past few nights of denying them the pleasure they both desired were foolish.

Kincaid ripped off his cravat and vest, dropping them on the floor as he walked toward the mirror. He stumbled and landed on the bed instead. In his attempt to rise and tear off his boots, he only managed to fall backwards. He shut his eyes. His body begged to fall asleep, but his heart protested for him to rise again and make his way to Jacqueline. The thought of Jacqueline alone gave him new purpose, and he yanked off his boots and threw them near the chairs by the fire. Fortunately, his aim was off. If not, his finest footwear would be kindling. Then he would have had to use his winnings to purchase new footwear.

He pushed himself off the bed to rescue his boots. He didn't need any sparks to land on them. Kincaid bent over to retrieve them when he noticed movement in a chair. A white billowing garment grabbed his attention. He closed his eyes and reopened one of them, trying to focus on the aberration.

Is there an angel in my bedchamber?

Kincaid wondered why an angel paid him a visit. Surely it was to help him capture the heart of the siren down the hall. What other reason could there be? He took a step forward but stopped when the angel moved.

Once she settled again, he moved until he stood above her. An arrogant smile spread across his face when he realized his angel was none other than the siren who haunted his dreams.

"Jacqueline?" Kincaid asked in awe.

She never answered him but kept on sleeping. Which was unusual for Jacqueline since usually the slightest sound startled her awake. He dropped to his knees before her. How was the lady an angel who also possessed the traits of a temptress? She lay curled in the chair with her head resting on her arm and the cushion of the chair. Her other arm dangled across her stomach. He reached out to slide his palm against hers. She mumbled in her sleep, and he swore it was his name. His gaze traveled the length of her, and he burst out laughing at the monstrosity she'd adorned her body with.

The nightdress was fit for a nun. While it appeared demure and what any virginal young lady would wear, she only wore it for one reason alone. She thought it would keep him from trying to seduce her when, in fact, it only invited him to unwrap her. For he knew already what lay beneath. A most fetching sight indeed. Kincaid released her hand and went to work on the buttons keeping him from seeing Jacqueline in all her glory.

Why else would she wait in his bedchamber if not for spending the night in his arms? Since he refused to visit her bed, she'd come to him. Once he untied the ribbon, he spread her robe to find his angel wearing a simple nightgown decorated with tiny bows on the shoulders straps and covering the trim above her breasts. He traced his fingers across the bows, grazing her soft skin. She felt heavenly.

He'd missed her these past few nights. Not only the joining of their bodies, but the stolen moments he spent holding her while they whispered their fears and greatest dreams. He fell under her spell in those magical instants and wanted to spend a lifetime reliving those moments over and over again. If only he could convince her to share his dreams. While she held herself back, perhaps instead of holding out on her, he should indulge her wishes spent underneath each other's bedsheets.

The most magnificent dream wrapped Jacqueline in its cocoon. Griffen caressed her with the gentlest of touches, each one softer than the last. A heavy desire spread through her, one that ached for him to stop his teasing. He pulled the ribbons loose on the straps of her nightgown, releasing them one by one. They dropped from her shoulders, and his lips replaced the soft fabric. He started at one shoulder and trailed down her chest to the bow between her breasts. Once he reached there, he paused, waiting.

"Griffen," Jacqueline moaned in her sleep.

He trailed his lips higher to the other shoulder, lighting her soul on fire, then moved back down to the bow between her breasts. He paused again. She grew impatient and dragged her lids open to find him staring intently at her. She shivered from his passionate gaze. Not once dropping her gaze, he sank his teeth into the ribbon and pulled it loose, gaping her gown wide open. Her body trembled with anticipation for him to continue his seduction. Her conscience pleaded with her to confront him while her body begged him to finish seducing her.

Would one more night of pleasure cause any harm?

One more night? What was she thinking? She kicked her legs out, knocking Griffen backwards. Jacqueline scrambled to her feet, pulling her nightwear around her. Griffen struggled to rise and slid back down until he sprawled across the floor. When he attempted again but fell back instead, he spread out. Glaring down at Griffen, Jacqueline retied the bows and buttoned her nightdress again.

"What is the matter, my love? I only attempted to help make you more comfortable for our bed," Griffen slurred.

"You are sloshed," Jacqueline hissed in exasperation.

He winked at her. "Perhaps. Just a smidge." He attempted to hold up his thumb and forefinger, showing how drunk he might be.

She stood over him with her hands planted on her hips. Griffen mused over how she'd often displayed her displeasure with him with the same pose lately. He wondered what infuriated her now.

"First of all, you are smashed. Second, it is not our bed, but yours. There will never be our bed. Third, I didn't come here to partake in a lovemaking session, but to convince you to wait before asking for my hand. I need time."

Griffen placed his hands behind his head and closed his eyes. "Time for what, my dear?"

"Time for..."

"Mmm," Griffen murmured before snoring.

"Oof." Jacqueline stomped her foot. He had the nerve to fall asleep on her. The drunken buffoon.

However, the behavior was unlike him. He was primmer and more proper than the most matronly lady of the ton. His behavior tonight was from the influence of the gentlemen of her family. Duncan, to be exact. However, she couldn't blame him because Duncan and Selina had left for Scotland soon after they spoke their wedding vows. And the married gentlemen stayed near their wives' sides until retiring for the evening. That left only her cousin Lucas and Graham Worthington to encourage him in his overindulgence. There had to be another reason for his inebriated state than an evening spent playing cards.

She tapped her foot against his side, trying to jar him awake. But he wouldn't budge. His snores grew louder. It would appear her visit to convince him to stay quiet was a waste. She gazed down at him, her heart softening as she watched him sleep. Even in his drunken state, Griffen endeared himself to her. Jacqueline only wanted to take care of him.

She pulled the quilt from the bed and covered him. Then grabbing the pillow, she knelt by his side and slid it underneath his head. Jacqueline brushed his hair from his eyes and trailed her fingers across his cheek. She bent her head and gently kissed his lips.

Then she whispered the one thing she could no longer deny. "Sweet dreams, my love."

~~~~~

Kincaid stretched his aching limbs. It was the worst sleep he'd had in a long while. His visit thus far had been most pleasant. However, his sleep last night was torturous, except for his tantalizing dreams. He dreamed of Jacqueline in a virginal gown with little bows. A tempting package for him to unwrap. He rolled over, reaching for her, but encountered the leg of a chair.

What?

He sat up, noticing why he'd had an ill night. Instead of a comfortable mattress, he'd endured the evening in a makeshift bed on the floor. Then he remembered how his evening had ended.

A drunken card game and winning a heavy pot to finding an angel awaiting his return once he reached his bedchamber. Not just any angel but Jacqueline. However, before he passed out, he'd angered her. He couldn't remember why, though.
~~~~~

He pulled himself off the floor and staggered toward his bed before collapsing again. Perhaps when he awakened later, it would all return to him. For now, he needed more sleep for his appointment with Colebourne to be a success. Kincaid drifted back to his dream of undressing Jacqueline and kissing her frown away.

Chapter Three

Colebourne strolled through the parlor nestled in the middle of the manor and settled in a chair near the window. He'd designed this room for his late wife to enjoy. They'd spent many hours together in the peaceful sanctuary as a family when Lucas was younger. He'd installed French doors that opened up to the rose garden. Olivia had taken to having her afternoon tea on the small terrace outside. On days like today, with the rain falling, she would laugh off the dread and throw open the window, allowing the roses' perfume to fill the room. The memories brought a smile to his face, easing the ache he felt at missing her.

It was where he knew he would find Olivia's sister, Susanna, and her husband, Ramsay. Susanna was his cohort in his matchmaking madness. She had opened the window, and a soft breeze wafted through. The fragrance of the roses and the melody of the rain falling lightly set the mood for the dilemma he needed to discuss with Susanna.

His latest match confused him on which course to take. The liberties he allowed Kincaid with Jacqueline had continued for too long. It must end with their marriage or he needed to send Kincaid away and settle Jacqueline with another gentleman. Even though it was his intention for them to wed, the length of their affair, if continued, would only lead to a scandal. How no one had discovered their affair yet was still a mystery. But if they weren't careful, Jacqueline could find herself in a motherly way.

They must make this match happen sooner than the others. It wasn't as if Kincaid hadn't offered for Jacqueline's hand in marriage; Colebourne had overheard the proposals on many occasions. His niece no doubt resisted the gentleman's offer because of her fear of losing Kincaid, as she had her parents. The most tragic loss had uprooted her life and forced her out of her comfortable environment. Jacqueline had adjusted well to the move, but she thought she had to step into her mother's shoes to fill the void with her two younger sisters, even mothering her cousin Gemma and Abigail Cason.

Each girl had reacted to her loss in a different manner. However, Jacqueline had been older, and the loss not only kept her from accepting Kincaid's offer of marriage, but she also refused to lose her independence. An independence Colebourne had encouraged since she came to live with him, one that Kincaid would also encourage her to hold. However, Jacqueline refused to hold faith in Kincaid's character.

It confused Colebourne. Kincaid was one of the most upstanding gentlemen in the ton. His strict structure of walking the straight and narrow, his polite mannerisms, his pursuit of knowledge, and his uncanny ability not to have any rumors of nefarious behavior attached to his name—it all kept him on many mothers' list of the ton's marital prospects. However, his depleted funds kept the fathers of the ton refusing a match.

Even with the knowledge Colebourne held of Kincaid's past disreputable acts and the reason behind his destitute standings, he still believed him the most favorable prospect for Jacqueline. Yes, at one time, Kincaid had involved himself with reckless behavior. However, before his name was whispered on the gossipmongers' tongues, Colebourne had aided him with an escape. And for years, Kincaid had repaid his debt whenever Colebourne requested it of him. Once he had noticed the attraction simmering between Kincaid and Jacqueline, Colebourne realized the need to clear the debt. But when Kincaid didn't appear at breakfast or their appointment scheduled, it left Colebourne in doubt of the match.

Susanna looked up from her needlework. "Did your meeting progress as planned with Lord Kincaid?"

Colebourne tapped his fingers on the arm of the chair. "He never showed."

Ramsay laughed and continued with his reading.

"Oh, dear. I thought perhaps he went for a morning ride, explaining his absence from breakfast since the rain stopped for a while. He has displayed his restlessness with the confinement since the wedding. Did he change his mind and leave early?"

"No. His horse still rests in the stables. I inquired of his whereabouts with Oakes, and he informed me that Kincaid has yet to rise for the day."

Susanna raised her brows. "That sort of behavior is out of character for Lord Kincaid."

"Not considering the late night he spent with Lucas and Graham. The card game continued into the early morning hours, and they consumed a two bottles of my best brandy. Kincaid claimed victory and won a sizable pot to keep him afloat for a couple of months."

"Good for the lad," Ramsay interjected.

Susanna frowned at her husband before turning her attention back to Theo. "I thought Lord Kincaid did not indulge in gambling or other vices."

Ramsay harrumphed. "If he is any red-blooded male, then he indulges in all vices."

Susanna narrowed her gaze at her husband again, not only for interrupting her but for his comments, too.

Colebourne laughed at Ramsay. There was much truth behind the remarks. "He does from time to time. However, nothing to draw the notice of others. And only in private gatherings among his friends. I am afraid this rain has pushed the gentlemen into overindulging in said vices."

Susanna set her needlework to the side. "Then I must plan some entertainments to keep them occupied with the other guests. Since this rain continues, after dinner this evening, we shall enjoy an evening of parlor games. Charades, I think." A sparkle lit her eyes at the different possibilities of grouping the teams.

"Do you have a plan?" Colebourne asked.

Susanna laughed. "One is formulating as we speak."

"Excellent. We must speed this courtship along. Oakes informed me of how Kincaid and Jacqueline are reckless with their affections. A few servants have noted them kissing and meeting alone without a chaperone. While I permit the girls certain freedoms not allowed in society, I do so with the trust of them not stepping over the lines of decency. If we are not careful, the rumors will leak, forcing them into a union. When I started this journey, it was for none of them to become forced into a marriage but to find their soul mates, as I had found mine with Olivia. But Jacqueline is riding the fence of having her virtue come into question."

Susanna nodded. "I understand. What you have set out to accomplish is remarkable. You have succeeded in four excellent matches. Your fifth match will find success, too. No matter how we must rush to make it happen."

"I know you wish to return home for the holidays and to welcome Selina into your family once she and Duncan return from their wedding trip. If you could hold off until after the fox hunt, I would greatly appreciate it."

"Of course we will. Will you offer Kincaid an audience after he awakens and realizes his blunder?"

Colebourne looked outside once more, pondering Susanna's question before answering. He glanced back toward her. "I am undecided."

"'Tis most simple. Make the bloke wait. Inform him of your indecision at considering a business partnership with his ineptitude for not arriving for a scheduled meeting. Make Kincaid stress over his predicament, forcing him to pursue Jacqueline with more determination." Ramsay offered a convincing argument.

Colebourne smiled. "I knew you would earn your stay, eventually."

Ramsay harrumphed. "You are lucky I do not send you a bill for my wife's matchmaking services."

"I think it has been a fair trade. Even though you overstep your bounds by having Cook supply you with extra treats not shared with others."

Ramsay chuckled. "'Tis not my fault your staff's loyalties lie with me and not you."

A devious gleam shone in Colebourne's eyes. "Well, I shall return the favor when I visit your castle for the holidays."

Susanna shook her head over their bantering. "You two are shameful."

An adequate term to describe the bond of their friendship.

Chapter Four

Kincaid scrambled out of the bedchamber and into the hallway, pulling on his suit coat behind him. He had overslept, missing breakfast and his meeting with Colebourne. He rushed down the stairs and into the dining area, hoping to catch the duke at luncheon. Instead, he walked into a room filled with ladies who were gathered around the table and enjoying a pot of tea.

Jacqueline's, Lady Forrester's, Lady Worthington's, and the Worthington daughters' sparkling laughter stopped at his appearance, and their curious gazes paused him in his tracks. He gulped and ran his hand through his hair. While the other ladies held a curious yet humorous expression at his predicament, Jacqueline's gaze held a mixture of disappointment and longing. An emotion he was quite familiar with.

"Lord Kincaid, we missed you at breakfast and lunch," Lady Forrester greeted him.

"Yes, well, I was… That is…"

"No worry. We dined buffet style and much remains. Please gather a plate. Since there is an empty seat next to Jacqueline, you may sit there." Lady Forrester fluttered her hand toward the food.

Kincaid glanced toward Jacqueline, but she avoided his gaze. He longed to sit next to her, but he must speak with Colebourne before his opportunity slipped from his grasp. "While I find Lady Jacqueline's company charming, I am afraid I must decline. I am late for my meeting with Colebourne."

Lady Forrester tilted her head. "No, my lord, you had one. However, when you neglected to appear for the time Colebourne allotted you, he revoked his offer. Now, he is enjoying a ride with my husband and won't return until dinner. Your best option is to enjoy the afternoon meal in our company."

"I accidentally overslept," Kincaid muttered an excuse. Even though it was pointless. It only displayed his weakness in front of the ladies present.

"An affliction my son must have suffered from, too," Lady Worthington declared.

"And what affliction might that be, Mother?" Graham Worthington strolled into the dining room with Gray. He walked to his mother's side and kissed her on the cheek.

Lady Worthington swatted his arm, shaking her head at his antics. "Rising at a late hour and missing time spent with your family," she reprimanded him.

"Time spent with these brats?" Worth tugged on Eden's and Noel Worthington's braids.

Eden glared her annoyance at Worth while trying to bite back a smile, and Noel giggled at his teasing. Worth sauntered over to the buffet, filled a plate, and returned to sit across the table from his sisters. They kept a friendly banter passing between them while he ate.

Kincaid stayed rooted to the spot, deciding what action he should take. In the end, he sighed in resignation. There wasn't much else for him to do but enjoy the meal with the present company. He couldn't chase after Colebourne since he didn't know which route he'd taken for his ride. After his evening spent over-imbibing, riding a horse around the countryside for the afternoon didn't sit well with him. No. He would bide his time and present his case to the duke after he profusely apologized for his absence. He turned to the buffet to fill his own plate and sat next to Jacqueline, who ignored his presence once again.

"In Worth's and Kincaid's defense, the blame lies at my feet. I fear I allowed them to overindulge in the late evening's entertainments," Gray apologized in between bites.

"What entertainments?" Noel asked innocently.

Lady Worthington and Lady Forrester spoke at once.

"Lucas—"

"Lord Gray—"

Gray winced. "My apologies."

Worth laughed and winked at his sister. "Only a card game."

"Oh. I thought perhaps it was the overindulgence of the duke's liquor," Noel continued in an innocent tone.

"Noel!" Lady Worthington's sharp warning echoed around them.

"Well, Mother, I only speak the truth. You can still smell it on Graham's breath."

The table erupted into laughter at Noel's observation. Lady Worthington may try to protect her daughters from a gentleman's vices, but after a childhood spent in the environment of an overindulged father, it was useless. It was difficult for a parent to protect their children, especially if one of them was a deprived degenerate.

The gentlemen continued to eat their lunch while the conversation flowed around the table. Kincaid kept quiet, observing Jacqueline with her family and friends. It didn't bother him when she ignored him. It was for the best. The conversation he wished to have with her was one he couldn't have with the party involved. He didn't even try to hold her hand. She'd made her feelings clear, and he didn't want to push his luck this afternoon. He'd already failed with Colebourne and had no wish to fail with her, too.

She was lovely, with her face animated as she watched the teasing banter of the Worthington clan. She even threw her own taunts into the mix, at ease in the exchange. While Jacqueline held a more serious nature than her sisters, she still enjoyed herself to the fullest in life. Her curiosity was the trait he most admired and what drew him to her.

He lost himself, remembering their first kiss.

He discovered the secret passageways by accident and went exploring one night three years ago during his stay. Jacqueline was returning from the library when he came across her. She carried an armful of books and ran into him, knocking the books from her hands. They both bent to the ground and knocked heads. As he moaned and rubbed his head, Jacqueline's laughter took him by surprise. He expected a lecture, only ever seeing the side of her proper behavior. However, her bubbling amusement invaded his senses. He wished to hear more.

After gathering the books, he helped her rise, holding her hand and refusing to relinquish it when a spark spread from her fingertips to his. He drew her near and lowered his head, capturing her lips under his. Instead of a slap across the face for taking such liberties, she only moaned, stepping up on her tiptoes to deepen the kiss. Her innocence exploded on his tongue with each brush. Nothing so exquisite had passed between his lips before, and he craved the sweet sensation.

When he stepped back to apologize, she stopped him with a question, shocking him. "Does a man and a woman only kiss each other on the lips?"

Before he could stammer a reply, she blushed a dark shade of red and scurried off, leaving him with a hard cock and a dire urge to show Lady Jacqueline exactly where else a man kissed a woman.

It hadn't been long after their stolen encounter that she'd granted him his wish. Her curiosity only flourished each time they made love.

"Do you not agree, Lord Kincaid?" Lady Forrester's question invaded his memories.

He cleared his throat, forcing his thoughts away. They were not ones to have at the dining table with innocent ladies. "I apologize. My thoughts distracted my attention. What am I agreeing to?"

"How a round of charades after dinner will be an excellent diversion to the dreary weather."

Gray and Worth moaned their disapproval. However, Kincaid wasn't in the position to do so. He had watched the influence Lady Forrester had over the Colebourne household and knew if he could charm her, then he would soon fall into the duke's good graces once again. "Yes. A most excellent diversion. I am looking forward to the entertainment after dinner."

Lady Forrester's devious grin lit her face. "I knew you would agree."

Kincaid nodded his understanding at the lady's unspoken declaration. However, his agreement didn't appease the lady sitting next to him. She only tsked her disapproval. Which in return made Kincaid smile. With one small turn of a conversation, he had placed himself in favor once again.

"Where is Abigail?" Gray asked, changing the topic.

"She is sitting with Gemma while Gemma rests," Lady Forrester answered.

Gray placed his napkin on the table before rising. "I think I will visit with them."

"If I am to spend time with my family, where is Maggie?" Worth asked.

"Reese and Evelyn have taken Maggie with them to visit the Sinclairs for the afternoon. They waited for you to join them, but when you remained in bed, they left without you," Lady Worthington explained.

Worth nodded. "I think I will ride to Sinclair's estate. Do you want to join me, Kincaid?"

"Not this time. I must work on my correspondence this afternoon."

"Very well. I will see everyone at dinner."

After Worth departed, the rest of the other ladies made their excuses, leaving Kincaid alone with Jacqueline and Lady Forrester. Kincaid sipped at his tea, thinking of a topic of conversation to share with the ladies. However, luck swung again back toward him when a servant entered, needing Lady Forrester's assistance in a decision for the household, leaving him alone with Jacqueline.

As soon as Aunt Susanna left, Jacqueline tried to rise, but Kincaid reached out, grasping her arm. She looked down at his strong fingers wrapped around her sleeve. His touch gentled under her stare. She fought with her emotions. When he sat next to her, she'd resisted his presence to the best of her ability. And failed miserably. Kincaid's disappointment in missing his meeting with Uncle Theo had settled heavily in her heart. She knew how important it was to him to have her uncle's backing. Jacqueline didn't know the full extent of his financial downfall, but if Uncle Theo showed his support in Kincaid's business venture, then others would fall behind it to make it successful.

His hand slid down, and he intertwined their fingers. Kincaid's mere touch soothed her troubled thoughts. When she left him lying on the floor, she had returned to her empty bed and lain awake until the sun rose before falling into a restless sleep. The same question kept playing over and over. Why did she refuse to accept his love?

Jacqueline sat back down at the tug of his hand. She was powerless in resisting him.

"Jacqueline, can we talk?"

"What is there to discuss? We are at an impasse. I have refused your offer, and you refuse to abide by my wishes."

"That is because your reasoning is absurd and you are stubbornly resisting what is so plainly obvious," Kincaid argued.

Jacqueline yanked her hand away. "And what is that, Lord Kincaid?"

Kincaid sighed. Instead of coaxing Jacqueline into a pleasant conversation, he'd ignited her temper instead. How could he turn this around to his advantage? Before he could reason with Jacqueline, the servants entered to clear away the luncheon, followed by Lady Forrester.

"Thank you, Lady Jacqueline, for accepting my offer for a walk around the garden. I will finish my tea and converse with Lady Forrester while you gather your bonnet." He stood and held out his hand, helping her rise from the chair.

Jacqueline fumed at his forwardness and wanted to swipe the smug look from his face. His comment forced her to accept his unspoken plea. As much as she wished to defy how he cornered her, Aunt Susanna wouldn't allow her to snub the viscount.

"I shall return shortly," Jacqueline answered in her sweetest voice.

Kincaid watched Jacqueline leave and chuckled at her reaction. Her singsong acceptance didn't fool him for a bit. She was furious at him for trapping her into a walk, but he would use this opportunity to his full advantage.

Lady Forrester resumed her seat. "Does something amuse you, Lord Kincaid?"

He settled back in the chair. "She is in quite a snit, is she not?"

She reached to pour herself another cup of tea. "Yes, she is. And you find humor in this?"

"Why, yes, I do."

Lady Forrester observed Lord Kincaid with interest. "Your behavior is quite peculiar, my lord."

He chuckled. "Actually, it is quite fitting for the circumstances, Lady Forrester."

"How so?"

Jacqueline appeared in the doorway, interrupting their conversation. However, Kincaid dangled a comment toward Lady Forrester to leave her wondering. "It falls nicely into my plans."

Jacqueline tied her bonnet. "What falls nicely into your plans?"

"Why, you, my love." He placed her hand in the crook of his arm and led them outdoors, away from prying ears.

"And those plans would entail what, exactly?"

"At the present, a pleasant walk with a charming companion on a glorious afternoon. Thankfully, the weather has given us a break from its misery."

"We are far enough away. You can give up on your false pretense of polite conversation."

Kincaid laughed. "Not only are you in a snit but prickly, too. A side of your character I have yet to experience. I must say I enjoy it immensely."

"I am not in a snit. Nor am I prickly," Jacqueline denied.

Kincaid pulled them behind a tree, drawing Jacqueline into his arms. He bent his head and kissed the corner of her lips. "Yes, you are, my love."

Jacqueline tried to resist sighing from his featherlight kiss, but his teasing softened her composure and a sigh escaped. Not only a sigh, but her hands slid around his neck and into his soft hair.

Kincaid needed no other encouragement. His lips coaxed hers to open, and he ravished her mouth like a man starved. Jacqueline tightened her grip on his hair, and he pressed himself closer. His tongue stroked hers, lighting the spark of their need. As the kiss continued, Jacqueline grew softer in his arms.

"Jacqueline, I need you."

Jacqueline tasted Kincaid's need from his kisses. It matched her own. She should put a halt to them, but they were too delicious to stop. She only craved more of them. When had their relationship changed from the simple affair they both enjoyed into one that bordered on obsession?

Jacqueline gasped once she realized the truth and broke from the kiss. She had succumbed to the same affliction the rest of her family suffered from. The love she held for Kincaid bordered on madness.

Kincaid groaned at the loss of Jacqueline's sweet lips. He raised his gaze, noting her pale face. Suddenly, she pulled from his grasp and ducked under his arm, backing away. With each step she took, Jacqueline's eyes grew wider.

He took a step toward her. "Jacqueline?"

Her hand struck out to stop him from moving any closer. "Do not take another step," she ordered.

Kincaid stopped. "What is wrong?"

"Your kisses. What else?" Desperation clung to her answer.

An arrogant smile met her reaction. "They never bothered you before. And only a few seconds ago, you were sighing into them."

"Yes. Well, you caught me by surprise. I… That is…" Jacqueline growled. "Never mind."

"Ahh, love, why are you fighting our attraction?"

"You know why. 'Tis the very reason I came to your bedchamber last night."

"Ahh, so your visit was not a dream of mine."

"Pshh. I should have known you were too soused to remember."

Kincaid shrugged. He led her to believe he thought her a dream when in fact he remembered every detail of her visit. There wasn't a time in their relationship when he'd ever forgotten touching and kissing her. Any vision of Jacqueline seared itself into his memories to cherish for his lifetime. Even down to her covering him with a blanket and lying a pillow underneath his head. He might have fallen asleep, but he noticed her gentle care.

"Why did you pay me a late-night visit?"

"To convince you not to ask Uncle Theo for my hand in marriage yet."

"Yet?" Hope vibrated from his one spoken word.

"I only need a while longer to accept your proposal. To come to terms with losing my independence."

Kincaid moved closer toward Jacqueline. "I am not asking for you to give up any freedoms you have. I am only asking for your love, and in return, you shall have mine. Our marriage will be on our terms, not the terms of society. I would think after the time we have spent together, you would understand my character better. But as I can see, you consider me as a poor option. Literally."

She shook her head. "No. No. You misunderstand."

Kincaid shook his head. "No, I do not believe so. However, since I am the one who stole your virtue, you must accept our impending union. I am a gentleman who will correct my misstep. You have until Sunday before I confess my dishonor to your uncle. I had hoped for a different outcome, one without a scandal attached to it. But then our courtship screams scandal." Kincaid released a bitter laugh. "Courtship. I even failed at that attempt with you. Yet, the love I hold for you consumes my soul and gives me the breath to keep fighting until I conquer your heart and soul."

Kincaid strode away, leaving Jacqueline trembling from his declaration. His tone declared his intentions and spoke of a determined man who would take any lengths to accomplish his threat. Yet was it a threat or a proclamation of what he greatly desired? Jacqueline shivered as she thought about the gleam in his gaze when he spoke of the love he held for her. Never once while they lay in each other's arms had he ever declared his feelings for her. She thought their nights were only a way to ease the ache their bodies craved. A mutual affair of the body, not one of the heart.

Jacqueline slid onto a bench. When had the sneaky emotion of love crept into their affair? It had to have happened during the madness of watching the twins and Gemma marry when Jacqueline lowered her defenses to the emotion. When she watched Selina and Duncan wed, the walls she had erected around her heart came tumbling down. The walls might have fallen, but she kept a shield around her heart to guard her from the pain of losing Griffen one day. But was the shield also keeping her from loving him freely without worrying over the unknown? Nothing in life was guaranteed. She wasn't foolish enough to believe it was. Yet, she continued to protect her heart from suffering the heartache of losing someone she loved again.

She wanted to stomp her feet and give in to a child's tantrum. The path of where her life traveled was so unfair at times. Why must it change? Hadn't she suffered from enough change to last a lifetime? Now she stood on the precipice of losing Griffen's affections if she forced him to confront her uncle with their scandalous affair. But would he dare? He had much to lose by admitting his ungentlemanly behavior. Uncle Theo would withdraw his offer of a business partnership if he hadn't already, since Griffen had missed their meeting. He couldn't afford to anger her uncle. No. Jacqueline didn't believe he would.

With her newfound belief, Jacqueline rose and smoothed out her skirts before returning to the house. She would give Griffen a couple of days to wind down before continuing their affair. If she kept her distance, he would see the error of his threat and seek her forgiveness. She would continue her silent treatment throughout the meals because Aunt Susanna would continue to sit them together. And she would fill her days with her sisters and Gemma before they returned to their own homes. Soon, they would travel to Scotland to spend the holidays in Aunt Susanna's home. By then, Kincaid would travel in the opposite direction to his estate. Their affair must end once the weekend drew near. For now, she would seduce him until he fell to her demands.

Then, and only then, she might offer him his greatest wish.

Chapter Five

Kincaid stood in the open doorway, contemplating how to approach the duke. He'd kicked himself all afternoon for his failure. The fault lay with him, as much as he wished to place the blame on others. No one had forced him to drink into the early morning hours while playing cards. Even if he did win a bundle, it'd ended up costing him more than he wanted to admit. Not only financially but emotionally, too. He risked losing Jacqueline before he'd even won her love.

Kincaid hesitated. "Colebourne, may I have a word?"

Colebourne looked up from the papers on his desk, narrowing his gaze at the viscount. "You lost your chance when you failed to present yourself for our meeting."

Kincaid nodded. "I understand. At this time, I only wish to offer my apologies for my inconsideration. I hope in time I can redeem myself in your eyes and regain the respect I lost."

Colebourne harrumphed. "I do not give second chances."

"I hope to change your mind." Kincaid stood firm with false confidence. However, he refused to let the duke see otherwise.

"There is nothing to change. Your absence proved how unreliable of a partner you would be in a business venture. Even though you have repaid your debt with your loyal service over the years, I rarely go against my decisions once I make them."

"You stand correct. Also, I will continue to repay my debt of gratitude I owe you for coming to my aid. However, I am not trying to redeem myself for a business partnership."

Colebourne looked confused. "Why else would you seek my forgiveness?"

Kincaid's smile grew smugger. "Not why. But whom."

"Whom?"

Kincaid straightened his shoulders and puffed out his chest. "I wish for your blessing to wed Lady Jacqueline."

Colebourne laughed. "If I will not support your financial venture, why would I allow you to pursue my niece?"

"Because no other gentleman will love her as I do. I may not have the fortune your other wards have married into, but I love Jacqueline with all my heart and I will devote my life to her happiness. And I know for a fact that is your greatest wish for her."

Colebourne leaned back into his chair, scrutinizing Kincaid. "What the others lacked in confidence, you hold in spades. I will give you that, Kincaid. However, I cannot condone a courtship between the two of you with the status of your finances in the dire straits they are. Jacqueline, above all, deserves the same standing as her sisters and cousin. And you, Lord Kincaid, cannot provide her with what she needs the most."

Kincaid's eye gave a slight twitch, the only sign displaying how Colebourne's comments grated on his nerves. However, he refused to rise to the duke's bait. Let him believe he held no other avenues to pursue. Colebourne wasn't the only peer he'd approached to discuss his business venture with. He just happened to be the first. Kincaid felt he owed the duke the first opportunity to accept. As for Colebourne refusing him a chance to court Jacqueline, the threat was pure rubbish.

He realized the duke's matchmaking games during the house party he attended before the start of the season. Since then, he had taken a front-row seat, watching him manipulate one gentleman after another into marrying his wards. First Sinclair, then Worthington, followed by Ralston. Then, to get his son out of his betrothal agreement, he played his matchmaking games on his own nephew, Duncan Forrester. Each courtship filled with scandal. Even his own affair with Jacqueline was truly scandalous.

Kincaid recognized the signs of Colebourne's manipulations. Over the years, the duke had controlled him at every opportunity that presented itself. And Kincaid had done the duke's bidding. If not, Colebourne would have revealed the threat of his ultimate demise and ruined Kincaid.

However, he was confident Colebourne wouldn't expose the damaging evidence of Kincaid's shame. Even though the duke refused his offer for Jacqueline, he was underhandedly playing matchmaker with them. Kincaid only needed to play along, too.

"And if I can prove otherwise?" Kincaid asked.

"Then I will grant you permission to marry Jacqueline. But only if Jacqueline agrees," Colebourne conceded.

Kincaid nodded in agreement and turned to leave. He made it as far as the door when Colebourne made his next move.

"I have invited Lord Falcone to the hunt. He showed Jacqueline interest during the season and has requested to become better acquainted with her on his visit. I granted him permission."

Kincaid gripped the door handle. He didn't turn around. "And has Jacqueline shown the same interest in Lord Falcone?"

"She does not need to." Colebourne's message rang clear.

Kincaid opened the door and strode down the hallway. And he swore he heard Colebourne's cackle following him on his heels.

~~~~~

"Ladies, when the gentlemen finish their brandy, we shall divide into groups and play a game of charades," Lady Forrester announced.

"Oh, I do hope I get placed with Lord Kincaid. He is most divine," Lady Noel gushed.

Her sister, Eden, rolled her eyes. "You think every gentleman in England is most divine."

Noel laughed. "Well, they are. But Lord Kincaid most especially, with his ocean-filled eyes and wavy blond hair. Please excuse me, ladies. I want to plead my case to Lady Forrester to place me on his team. Wish me luck."

Eden waited for her sister to cross the room before she soothed her friend. "Pay Noel no mind. She holds no interest in Lord Kincaid other than to practice her flirtation skills."

Jacqueline had stiffened when Noel tittered on about Kincaid. She swung her head toward Eden, pretending indifference at the mention of the viscount. "Why would I mind?"

Eden tilted her head with an expression of *you do not fool me for a second.* "Perhaps because your interest lies with the handsome lord."

"Nonsense. Your sister is more than welcome to the viscount."

"My sister is an incorrigible flirt, and Lord Kincaid is the only available male who is not family for her to entertain herself with. And you are the one who speaks nonsense."

Jacqueline pinched her lips and turned her head to the side, watching the other ladies talk amongst themselves. Noel's carefree attitude
~~~~~

drew forth laughter from her sisters and Gemma. Had she ever been lighthearted and enjoyed herself without restrictions? With each passing year, her status as a lady past the debutante stage hindered her actions into behaving more like a lady on the shelf. Except for the stolen moments with Kincaid that brought forth a lightness in her soul she hadn't felt since she was a young girl.

"Jacqueline?"

"Mmm."

"Please forgive me for overstepping the bounds of our friendship," Eden apologized.

Jacqueline attempted a smile. "You haven't."

"I only thought we had grown closer over the past few months. I did not mean to upset you."

Jacqueline grabbed Eden's hand. "I am not upset. You are correct about Lord Kincaid. As much as I keep trying to deny how much he means to me, my heart refuses to listen."

Eden frowned. "Why fight your destiny?"

Jacqueline's only answer was a shrug. How could she answer her friend when she was clueless to the answer herself?

"Well, if you want my opinion."

A smile lit Jacqueline's face. "Do I have a choice?"

Eden laughed. "No."

"Then share your wisdom with me, my friend."

"I believe you should give Lord Kincaid a chance. Embrace your secret courtship and see where it leads. You might discover his love is the answer your heart yearns for."

"Very sound advice."

Eden nodded toward the door. "Perhaps you will follow it this evening."

Kincaid trailed into the drawing room behind the other gentlemen.

"Perhaps," Jacqueline murmured.

When her gaze connected with his, Kincaid collided into Gray and Worth, who had stopped when Aunt Susanna stepped in front of them. He recovered his balance but appeared ruffled by his misstep. Usually, Kincaid was an unflappable fellow, always in control. However, on this visit, he was anything but. His behavior was off-center and unpredictable. From late-night gambling and drinking to sleeping in late, missing appointments, and flustered mannerisms. Jacqueline was curious to know the reasons for his unusual behavior.

Her mere glance turned him into a bumbling fool who tripped over his own two feet. Kincaid spent another dinner enduring her silent treatment while she flirted with Worth. The desire in her gaze contradicted her words from this afternoon and the distance she kept between them. Jacqueline Holbrooke perplexed him with her mixed signals. He tried to show how indifferent he was to her rejection, but it took every ounce of his control not to scamper over to her like a lovesick pup.

"Pay attention, Kincaid," Gray muttered.

"You gentlemen will remain in the drawing room for the evening. Colebourne has asked for entertainments after dinner and we are playing charades," Lady Forrester ordered.

Gray and Worth groaned their disappointment, but Kincaid was more than thrilled at the chance of spending time in Jacqueline's company. When Lady Forrester winked at him, he knew the lady planned to partner him with Jacqueline. Why else would she be so adamant about them staying? The evening took a turn for the better. Kincaid nodded his acceptance and strode over to talk with Ralston before the games began.

~~~~~

Colebourne sauntered over next to Susanna. "The boy is beyond smitten."

Susanna's eyes twinkled. "Did you see how he stumbled when Jacqueline set her gaze on him?"

"Ahh, I love when they fall in the name of love. Do you have them partnered together?"

"Yes. However, Lady Noel has requested to be in Lord Kincaid's group."

Colebourne glanced shrewdly at Jacqueline, Kincaid, and Lady Noel. "And Jacqueline continued with her silent treatment toward Kincaid during dinner. You need to make a switch. Place Lady Noel and Kincaid in the same group, and we shall see how Jacqueline reacts to their partnership."

Susanna tsked. "So devious, Colebourne."

Colebourne winked. "One must be in this matchmaking madness."

~~~~~

Kincaid didn't know how he ended up partnered with Lady Noel during the game of charades. While she was charming, her endless excitable chatter made the evening drag on without an end in sight. His assumption of becoming paired with Jacqueline had been wrong. Lady Forrester had fooled him with her wink.

His gaze drifted across the room once again to stare at Jacqueline. Before it landed on her, he encountered Colebourne's arrogant smirk. The duke wouldn't make Kincaid's pursuit of Jacqueline easy. No. His goal was to make Kincaid prove himself worthy of Jacqueline's love. A task Kincaid planned to succeed at.

"Is this not the most enjoyable pastime?" Lady Noel asked.

Kincaid gave her a patient smile. It wasn't the poor girl's fault for his foul mood. It was Colebourne's. Even though she stared at him with adoring eyes, he only treated her as one would a younger sister. It was moments like these he was thankful he had none.

"Yes, and you play the game brilliantly."

Lady Noel blushed at his compliment. "My family plays charades every chance we get for entertainment."

"That explains how apt you are at guessing the clues. I am most impressed."

Noel's blush darkened. She bent her head and looked at him coyly from between her lashes. "Thank you, Lord Kincaid."

He wanted to groan at her obvious display of flirtation. It wasn't his intention to encourage the miss. He only wished to keep the atmosphere pleasant and to pass the evening as swiftly as possible. Then he could steal a moment alone with Jacqueline. He wished to smooth over his blunt behavior from their walk in the garden and hoped she'd forgiven him. While he meant every word, he hadn't meant to speak so harshly to her. However, his frustration kept mounting day by day. At every turn, an obstacle stood in the way of achieving his dreams.

Kincaid shifted his attention away from Noel to seek Jacqueline again. This time, he found her gaze fastened on him. Her eyes narrowed and her lips puckered as if she'd sucked on a sour lemon. She kept glancing back and forth between him and Noel.

Is my angel jealous?

He decided to put his theory to the test. Kincaid leaned as close as possible to Lady Noel, where no one could question his impropriety, and whispered in her ear.

Lady Noel's eyes widened at his suggestion. "Yes. I would love to!"

She drew everyone's attention to them. To Jacqueline, it would appear as if he'd asked to spend time with Lady Noel, but he'd actually asked the lady to perform the next charade. He gave Noel a charming smile and leaned back in the chair. When he glanced back at Jacqueline, he arched his brow and gave her a nod.

Soon she unraveled, proving his point. Jealousy rolled off the love of his life as he regarded another lady with his charm. From across the room, he watched her grit her teeth and clench her hands. Smoothing things over with Jacqueline wouldn't happen this evening, but it was worth it to see her reaction.

As much as she denied her feelings toward him, her jealousy proved otherwise.

Chapter Six

The longer Jacqueline focused on Kincaid, the more agitated she became. Why, the bounder flirted with Lady Noel. Kincaid never flirted. He thought himself too above the simple act. She should know. Jacqueline had attempted to gain his attention many times when she was younger. And each time, he'd ignored her and showed no interest. It wasn't until she threw herself at him in the secret passageway that he'd taken any interest. Then neither one of them could deny the attraction that sizzled between them.

"What did he whisper in her ear to draw such a reaction?" Jacqueline muttered under her breath.

"I beg your pardon?" Sinclair asked.

Jacqueline stilled. Had she spoken aloud?

"Yes, and you still are," Sinclair quipped.

Jacqueline closed her eyes in exasperation with herself. He was making her lose her mind.

"Who?"

Jacqueline swung around and found Sinclair regarding her with a troubled stare. "Who?"

Sinclair gave her a pensive stare. "Yes. Who is making you lose your mind?"

"Nobody."

"Mmm. So you say. But I think a certain gentleman has you in knots, my dear friend."

"Nonsense. No gentleman holds my interest. Also, I refuse to fall into the same trap as my sisters."

Sinclair shrugged. "Perhaps you already have."

Jacqueline refused to answer. She gave him her best *mind your own business* stare, but he only laughed.

"If it is any consolation, I feel Kincaid is worthy of your love and the best mate for you. I give my approval."

Jacqueline glanced around to see if anyone had overheard their conversation. When she noticed no one paid them any mind, she tried to convince Sinclair how wrong he was on his assumption. "I have no clue to what you are implying."

Sinclair stretched out his legs and laughed. "If that is how you wish to continue, then I concede. However, please hear me out. All right?"

Jacqueline nodded.

"Love is rare. The members of this family who have embraced the emotion are lucky souls. Do not let your fear or your worries stop you from embracing your own happily ever after. If so, you will regret losing him. There are few blokes I respect and give my seal of approval to. But Kincaid is one gentleman I will give that honor to. Give him a chance to prove himself. I promise you will not suffer disappointment."

Tears rushed to Jacqueline's eyes at Sinclair's speech. Through the years, they'd formed a close friendship, and when he married her younger sister, Charlie, in the spring, their bond had only strengthened. For Sinclair to hold a high opinion of Kincaid only reaffirmed the gentleman's character.

"Why do you assume Kincaid is the gentleman I fancy?"

Sinclair coughed into his hand. "I might have seen him using the secret passageway when I was pursuing your sister."

Jacqueline arched a brow. "Do you not mean to imply when you scandalously ruined Charlie?"

Sinclair arched a brow in return. "And the same act Kincaid is guilty of himself?"

Jacqueline sighed. "Fine, you are correct. Kincaid has me tied in knots. But look at him." Jacqueline discreetly pointed across the room. "He is on to charming his next conquest."

Sinclair laughed. "Believe me, he is not. I have never seen another gentleman grimace so much as Kincaid has this evening sitting next to Lady Noel."

"Mmm." Jacqueline had observed a different scene.

"I think Lord Kincaid is attempting to make you jealous. You have made him a desperate man indeed."

Jacqueline tilted her head, trying to see what Sinclair saw. When she noticed Kincaid's eye twitching at Lady Noel's giggles, she realized her brother-in-law was correct. "I see your point now."

"And my advice?"

"I will take it into consideration."

Sinclair patted her hands. "Excellent. Now shall we show these people how to win at this game?"

Jacqueline gave him a sparkling smile. "Yes, let us show them how."

Kincaid had failed. He attempted to make Jacqueline jealous, yet he suffered from the green-eyed monster. Once again, she favored Sinclair with her attention. Lady Forrester had partnered them together for charades, but did they need to sit so close together? When Sinclair offered her comfort,

Kincaid wanted to storm across the drawing room and shove him away. His thoughts led him down an irrational path. Sinclair held devotion to only one woman alone, his wife, Charlie. Kincaid had witnessed their love and knew Sinclair only held a brotherly affection for Jacqueline. His reaction was from losing Jacqueline's affection over the past week.

When Jacqueline and Sinclair stood up to perform the next charade, they drew forth a round of laughter. Jacqueline no longer appeared upset, and instead joy radiated from her. When their teammates guessed the correct answer, Sinclair wrapped Jacqueline in a hug and swung her around. Soon her sisters joined in the celebration. Sinclair stepped back as they twirled around in a circle. Kincaid couldn't help but chuckle at their childlike exuberance.

"It would appear we have lost, Lord Kincaid."

Kincaid turned toward Lady Noel, taking notice of her pleased expression as she gazed at the Holbrooke sisters celebrating. "So we have. However, you are a good sport. Perhaps we will beat them next time."

Lady Noel nodded and smiled at him. "Perhaps we will. Have a pleasant evening, my lord."

Kincaid rose and helped her from the chair. "You too, my lady."

Kincaid smiled, watching Lady Noel join the other ladies. She placed a hand on Jacqueline's arm, congratulating her. Perhaps he'd thought unkindly of the young miss. There was more to her character than a silly debutante. Any gentleman who set out to win Lady Noel's heart would be a lucky bastard indeed. His gaze encountered Jacqueline, and she gifted him with a shy smile and a tilt of her head. The secret signal to visit her bedchamber.

He gulped. Was he forgiven? He tilted his head in agreement, and Jacqueline bit her bottom lip, nodding at his answer. Her look spoke volumes. And he would grasp at any sign from her because it proved she hadn't given up on him yet. Nor would he give her a chance to. His only purpose was to win Jacqueline's love.

A hand slapped him on the shoulder as Gray stepped up next to him. "Another round, Kincaid? I need to win my money back."

Kincaid never took his gaze off Jacqueline. When she overheard Gray, a doubtful expression crossed her features. However, he reassured her of his intentions. "No. I am turning in early. Perhaps another time."

Before Gray could change his mind, Kincaid strode off, wishing everyone a good evening. Once he entered the hallway, his stride quickened as he hurried to his bedchamber. He wanted to prepare himself for a night of loving Jacqueline. At least he didn't have a valet awaiting his return. Sometimes it was frustrating not having a servant to attend to him. However, it was only a minor setback. Soon his station would improve, and he could enjoy the luxuries in life again.

Kincaid stripped off his clothes and freshened himself with the water provided. He looked in the wardrobe and pulled on a fresh shirt and pants he could remove quickly. He threw a robe on, in case he met anyone in the secret passage. While he encountered no one whenever he snuck to her room, he knew he pressed his luck.

Kincaid paced back and forth as the minutes ticked away. He should have stuck around and waited for Jacqueline to retire first. After an hour passed, he decided he'd waited long enough. He would risk going to her bedchamber and hope her maid had retired for the evening.

When he turned toward the mirror, he stopped in his tracks. He didn't need to leave because she'd come to him. She stood against the mirror, wearing the nightgown from the night before. When she gained his attention, she untied the ribbons, and her robe fell around her feet. The tiny ribbons of her nightgown teased him. He needed no other encouragement.

His fingers trembled as he untied one ribbon after another. Her hair tumbled around his hands when she bent her head to watch him. With each ribbon, he revealed her softness. Silky. Sensuous. And very scandalous. Exactly the way he wanted her. No other way would do. He slid the garment off her shoulders, baring her before him. Jacqueline was exquisite.

Griffen tipped her chin up and gazed into eyes filled with passion that needed to be explored. He lifted her in his arms and lowered his head, taking her mouth slowly, savoring her sweetness. She tasted of the sugary candy she kept hidden in the stand next to her bed. His tongue licked along her lips before sliding inside to stroke alongside her tongue. He carried her over to the bed, not once breaking his lips from hers. After he laid her on the mattress, he stepped back and gazed down in wonder. Every time she lay before him, it was as precious as the first.

She stared at him with adoring eyes, dazed from their kisses. Her plump lips begged him to return his attention to them. Jacqueline's creamy skin glistened in the candlelight. Her breasts rose with each deep breath she claimed, and her nipples tightened when his eyes raked her form. He licked his lips, eager to suckle them while he caressed her generous curves. His gaze lowered, taking in her stomach and the flare of her hips. Hips his hands would cling to as he made love to her. Then there were her long limbs that would stretch around him and cling like a vine. His eyes traveled back up her legs to where his lips would claim the sweetest juice ever to pass between his lips.

He tore off his clothing, eager to join their bodies, to have their skin slide against one another. At his perusal, Jacqueline gave little whimpers of need. They fueled his desire, but he kept them waiting, drawing out the suspense of when their bodies would become one. When Jacqueline stretched out and shifted her legs apart, Kincaid was a fallen man. He could no longer resist the fetching goddess spread across his bed. Nor did he want to.

Jacqueline gasped when Griffen tugged her toward him with a determination she had never seen before. The fierceness in his gaze caused her to tremble. She eagerly waited for the touch of his caress and the stroke of his tongue against her quivering flesh. He gazed at her for an eternity, and she wantonly spread herself across the bed, with a need so fierce it no longer frightened her. Instead, she wished to embrace the unknown, no matter the consequences. As long as he never stopped his fascination.

When his hand stroked up her leg and spread her thighs apart, Jacqueline sighed in pleasure. However, he never lowered his head. Instead, his fingers teased her by drawing close, then deliberately trailing away. Her anticipation built into a frenzy, with her hips rising from the bed, seeking his touch. Griffen lowered his head, his tongue following his fingers, placing soft kisses on the insides of her thighs.

"Griffen," Jacqueline moaned.

Griffen refused to respond to her moans. His lips trailed a path of sin between her thighs. He inhaled the heady musk of her passion, but still, he denied them what they both desired, building on the temptation. With each rise of her hips, his lips were but a brush away from caressing her. The glistening dew of her wetness tempted him closer. Soon her hands dived into his hair, urging him closer. However, he kept plying her thighs with soft kisses, waiting for the moment when she fell apart without a single kiss.

He knew she rode the heady waves of pleasure. Her desperation was declared with each tightening of her fingers and how her thighs spread wider. Her moans and whispers begged him to pleasure her. Jacqueline shook beneath him, her moans growing louder, her mind floating toward abandoning her doubts.

Jacqueline couldn't stand the agony. Her body hungered for a mere touch or a kiss to slide over her wetness. Griffen held back from giving in to her demands, torturing her with his simple touch when her body craved his domination. He strung her out where she was ready to explode from the sheer anticipation. Why must he deny them?

When he spread her farther apart and hovered close, Jacqueline tried to press closer. But he held her thighs still with his fingers, gripping their softness. She watched him lick his lips. The slow caress of his tongue slid over their fullness. Then his smile turned wicked and a devilish glint shone from his eyes right before he blew a soft breath across her core.

"Ohhh." Her breathy moan echoed around the room.

He didn't stop at one. No, he tortured her with many. Each one different. Some of them were slow and lasted for seconds on end. Others were short blasts of a warm sensation of heaven, that teased her into a frenzy. In between stealing her senses, his tongue lingered, barely sliding across her wetness. She thought she imagined the gentle caress, but her body knew otherwise. Jacqueline was unraveling, falling over the edge only to soar again when his tongue struck out and eased the ache consuming her.

Griffen caught Jacqueline and devoured the flood of her desire. His ravenous mouth explored her hidden desires, demanding her submission. Each lash of his tongue claimed her soul. His relentless strokes sent her soaring again. When his fingers slid inside and drew forth more of her passion, she tightened around him, sending him to his knees. With each vibration of her need, he was on the verge of losing the control he tried to keep tightly contained. However, her soft moans, the sweet flavor on his tongue, and her body shaking around him urged him to join her.

Each time Jacqueline floated down from her release, Griffen strung another one out of her. She lost a piece of herself with each soar to paradise, only to feel more whole when she settled in Griffen's arms.

That evening, their lovemaking shifted into unknown territory. Each one was unsure of where their relationship lay, making it more desperate. Neither one of them wanted to lose the other. They were clueless about how to proceed. While indecision rested in the back of Jacqueline's thoughts, the sensations he drew with each kiss were all she needed.

Griffen rose above Jacqueline, and she wrapped her arms around him, drawing him into her body. He slid in with one long slow thrust, sending them spiraling into a higher existence they had never traveled to before. Their gazes clung to one another while their bodies became one. He wanted to whisper endearments of his love, but he didn't want to shake the connection they had settled in with their unspoken lovemaking. He drew on his patience and expressed his love with each kiss. Each caress. Each stroke. She had to see how much he adored her. How could she not?

Every emotion Griffen expressed with his lovemaking rushed through Jacqueline. He held back from declaring his love because he knew she wasn't ready to confront the truth of their relationship. She didn't deserve him, but she refused to release him. She tightened her grip, fearful he would slip through her arms. Her legs wrapped around his hips, and she pressed herself into him, clinging with need.

The agony of losing his love made Jaqueline feel desperate. Her kiss turned frantic with each pull of her lips. His body answered her cries of fear. With each thrust, they lost themselves in each other's souls.

Long after they reached satisfaction, Griffen kept placing soft kisses across her body, even once Jacqueline dozed in his arms. He would wake her soon. However, for now, he was more than satisfied with watching her sleep.

The angel of his dreams.

Chapter Seven

An awful churning sensation in her stomach jerked Jacqueline awake. She scrambled off the bed and ran to the chamber pot, where she bent over and lost the remains of her dinner. Her body protested at her every movement.

Once she finished, a set of comforting arms scooped her off the floor and carried her back to the bed. After lowering her against the pillows, Griffen wet a cloth and wiped around her mouth. Then he gathered another wet cloth and ran it across her forehead and along her neck. His gentle care soothed her into closing her eyes again.

"Jacqueline?"

Her light snores answered him, and he frowned over her sudden illness. One minute he woke her with light caresses. The next she hurried away to relieve her stomach. Griffen held his hand across her forehead, but her skin felt cool. She didn't have a fever. Perhaps the damp weather had made her ill. He hoped it was nothing dire.

He crawled back into bed next to her, drawing her in his embrace to keep a close watch over her. Griffen needed to wake her soon, so she could return to her bed before the servants started their day. She snuggled into him, muttering his name in her sleep. He tightened his arms around her, worry settling in. He was an insensitive oaf for making love to her while she was ill. Even though she displayed no other signs, he should have known of her illness.

"Do not regret what we just shared. I cannot stand it when you frown." Jacqueline's sleepy voice penetrated his thoughts.

Jacqueline reached up to smooth his frown away. She didn't understand why she had gotten sick, but she felt perfectly fine now. Something from dinner must have upset her stomach. Griffen's concern was touching. He was perfect.

Or most divine, as Noel referred to him. She quietly chuckled at Noel's description of Griffen.

Griffen's brows drew together in confusion. "And what causes your amusement?"

"I remembered Lady Noel's apt description of you after dinner and realized how correct she is in your character."

He groaned at the mention of the debutante's name. "Do I even dare to ask what that may be?"

Jacqueline giggled. "Mmm. Perhaps I shall keep her opinion to myself. I do not want to boost your ego and give you an edge in your pursuit."

Griffen smiled at her with arrogance. "That flattering, is it?"

Jacqueline's smile turned mysterious. "I shall never tell."

"No need to utter a word. For you to mention how it will boost my ego speaks of the compliment in itself."

Griffen laughed at Jacqueline's reaction. While trying to keep her secret, she'd divulged how flattering Lady Noel's opinion was. One in which Jacqueline herself must hold the same sentiment. He didn't need to hear the exact words. Her enjoyment warmed his heart, and he felt like they had reclaimed their connection away from all the matchmaking fuss.

He pulled her closer, placing a kiss on the top of her head. If only they could remain in the folds of their embrace. However, he must return

Jacqueline to her bedchamber before someone discovered them. He didn't want to force her into marriage, even though his greatest wish was to wed her.

"Love, we must get you returned to your room before your maid arrives."

Jacqueline sighed. She didn't want to leave Griffen's bed, or his arms, for that matter. But she must. Already a light ray of sunshine waited on the horizon to shine, and darkness rapidly faded away. Before she left, she wanted to know about his time spent with Noel Worthington. A bit of jealousy clung to her doubts over Griffen.

Jacqueline snuggled into his arms deeper, keeping her head against his chest so he wouldn't see her reaction. "Before I leave, will you answer a question for me?"

"Anything. Ask away."

"What did you whisper to Noel during charades?" Jacqueline asked.

Griffen couldn't help his reaction. His shoulders started shaking first, then his chest rumbled with the humor of the situation. She swatted at his chest and tried to pull away, but he only gathered her tighter. In his defense, her insecurity brought forth his own where Sinclair was concerned. Their doubts were absurd, yet it warmed his heart that Jacqueline felt threatened by Lady Noel.

He tipped her head up and placed a soft kiss on her lips. "Nothing of importance, my jealous minx."

"I am not jealous." Jacqueline pouted.

"Yes, you are. 'Tis most adorable."

Jacqueline huffed and tore herself away. She rose and dressed, fuming over how foolish she was for coming to his room when he was trifling with her emotions. Jealous? Even if that were the truth, she had a valid reason for her reaction. The more she fumed, the more frustrated she became. How dare he flirt so brazenly with another lady while she shared his bed? It only proved how ungentlemanly Lord Kincaid actually was. Did it not?

Griffen let Jacqueline finish dressing before soothing her insecurity. Who knew someone as confident as Jacqueline suffered from wasted emotions? However, she differed no more than him. His own jealousy over Sinclair lay proof of how one would question the validity of their companionship when they kept it hidden from others. It allowed doubt in the sincerity of their relationship to blossom. Before she returned to her bedchamber, Griffen must reassure Jacqueline of his devotion.

And to do that, she must finish getting dressed. Because he struggled to keep his hands to himself while she lay naked in his arms. After he made sure she suffered no more ill effects, he wanted to make love to her again. His visit drew close to an end. He needed to travel to his estate soon and didn't know when he would return. Nor did he have a plausible reason to visit. The duke had already made his position clear. He might have ended their previous agreement since Griffen had fulfilled his debt, but the duke wouldn't join him in his business venture. So he no longer had a reason to remain. After the hunt and dinner, Griffen must take his leave.

He hoped to wear down Jacqueline's resistance with his loving. They were both powerless to each other's kisses and soft caresses. If he continued with his onslaught of passionate affections, he could wear her down into accepting his marriage proposal. Because parting from her after this visit would be hellish torture. She was the other half of his soul. Jacqueline gave him the confidence to succeed. Without her in his life, he saw no need to accomplish a single goal. For she was the very reason he breathed.

Jacqueline tied the belt around her waist with a hard tug and strode to the mirror, determined to leave. Before she stomped into the secret passageway, his soft answer gave her pause.

"I told her she could perform the next charade since she found such amusement playing the game. 'Tis all."

Jacqueline slowly turned. Griffen stood next to the bed wearing nothing but a soft smile on his lips. She gulped at the sight. His gentle expression contradicted the arousal his body betrayed. Her mouth watered at his confident stance. She heard him explaining himself, but her fascination with his body kept her from learning his explanation. His need, on full display, was the only thing she understood. Her brazen thoughts overcame her senses. She wished to stroke her hand along his length and caress the firm steel in her palm. She licked her lips, remembering the taste of him.

Griffen groaned when Jacqueline slid her tongue across her lips. She didn't listen to a word he said, instead devouring him with her eyes. He glanced out the window to see if he could satisfy their needs. The night sky had disappeared and sunshine lit the countryside. Of all days, why must it stop raining? He sighed and gathered a sheet to wrap around his waist.

"Jacqueline," Griffen stressed.

"Mmm." Jacqueline raised her head in disappointment when Griffen covered himself.

"You, madam, are a temptation I must resist for now. Turn around and look outside."

Jacqueline turned her head to glimpse out the window. She wished he would drop the sheet to uncover himself. However, when she noted how light it was outside, Jacqueline realized she must return to her bedchamber with haste.

"Oh, no." She searched the floor for her slippers. "Why have you kept me so long?"

Griffen chuckled at her frazzled state. Even though she was the one who'd stood ogling him, he was to blame. "Because I could not bear to part from your beauty."

"Now is not the time for you to practice your charming nature. Help me find my slippers before I am caught," Jacqueline ordered.

"You find me charming?"

"Kincaid." Jacqueline growled her impatience

Griffen chuckled and strolled toward her, bending over to retrieve the slippers right in front of Jacqueline. He picked up each foot one at a time and slid the footwear onto her feet. Then he rose and gave Jacqueline a kiss she wouldn't forget. He wanted her to leave his bedchamber with memories of passion, not fraught with worry. She sighed into his kiss and relaxed with each soft whisper of his lips on hers. He teased her with his desire, then pulled away.

"Hurry. I will step into the hallway and cause a distraction if I see anyone on their way to your bedchamber." He stepped away and dropped the sheet, reaching for his trousers.

When Jacqueline didn't answer him and the mirror didn't open, he swung around. Only to find Jacqueline watching him again. Ahh, the minx made her intentions more than obvious. "Jacqueline?"

Why was she so easily distracted? She couldn't concentrate on a single thing. One minute she ordered him to find her slippers because she needed to hurry, and the next she stood there admiring his divine form. Oh, there was that darn word again.

She watched him pull on his robe, her last distraction covered. "Yes, an excellent idea." She peeked out into the secret passage and noticed the empty corridor. She rushed out and hurried to her bedchamber. It wasn't until she stood inside her room that she never...

"Well, she has finally returned, ladies. But one must question the reason for her delay?" Charlie asked.

Jacqueline's eyes widened when her sister spoke and her gaze wandered around, taking in her sisters, Gemma, and Abigail, all waiting for her. "I, um… That is… I am returning from the kitchen. I requested a pot of peppermint tea for breakfast to settle my stomach."

"Oh, you poor dear. Were you ill all night?" Abigail came to Jacqueline's side and helped her back to bed.

Once Abigail settled her under the covers, she nodded. She didn't dare try to offer any other excuses. Her sisters were too wise and would know she lied. It was best to stay silent and hope their curiosity would pass. However, once again, luck refused to stay on her side.

"Ill? Pshh. Not unless a ravished appearance is proof of sickness," Charlie quipped.

"Or when one's hair is in disarray," Evelyn added.

"Or swollen lips that were ravished repeatedly throughout the night," Gemma ended with a mischievous chuckle.

Abigail narrowed her gaze, and her head swiveled between Jacqueline and each lady who commented. "How dare you ladies? Jacqueline suffers from a stomach ailment and you want to accuse her of engaging in a scandalous tryst?"

"Yes," each lady answered simultaneously.

A blush warmed Jacqueline before she pulled the covers over her head. She'd lingered too long with Griffen. Now she must suffer the consequences. So much for him distracting any unwanted visitors. But he'd never had the chance because they were already waiting for her return. Now she could no longer hold their affair a secret. All of them except for Abigail would regard their courtship with stars in their eyes, believing Jacqueline and Kincaid would end their affair with a marriage. An ending not to Jacqueline's liking. *Or is it?*

"Jacqueline?" Abigail inquired.

She lowered the blanket, cringing with one eye open. "Yes?"

"Is there any truth behind their ramblings?"

"Perhaps."

Abigail sighed. "Not you, too. I had hoped you, of all the Holbrooke ladies, would have conducted a more proper courtship."

"Oh, this is so marvelous. Who is the lucky gentleman?" Gemma asked.

"Well, she does not have many options to choose from since most of the gentlemen present are members of our family. Which only leaves two eligible gentlemen for Jacqueline to choose from. One Graham Worthington or the most *divine* Griffen Kincaid. That is the apt description of Lord Kincaid, is it not, Jacqueline?" Charlie cackled.

"Jacqueline and Graham would make an unlikely couple. So, that rules out my brother-in-law," Evelyn answered.

"Which only leaves Lord Kincaid. A certain gentleman I saw Jacqueline sneak away with during the season at the Calderwood Ball. I thought I was mistaken, but it is now clear I was not." Gemma gasped. "You carried on an affair with him during the season. Why, you are the most scandalous of us all."

Jacqueline's blush refused to vanquish with each assumption. How she'd kept the affair hidden was a miracle upon itself. However, it must end now. She preferred not to discuss her circumstances with them, even though she knew they meant well. "Is there a reason for you invading my bedchamber this morning?"

"Nice try, sis. But you must answer the question on all of our minds. Is Kincaid most divine?" Charlie waggled her eyebrows, sending the ladies into a fit of giggles.

Jacqueline sighed. "Yes." Then she yanked the quilt back over her head.

Evelyn clapped her hands. "Oh, Jacqueline, we are so happy for you."

At her sister's joyous declaration, Jacqueline sat up in bed and rested against the headboard. She smoothed her hair down and straightened her clothing. "My relationship with Kincaid is not in the same regard you have found with your husbands. I have no wish to marry. We are in a beneficial arrangement that suits our needs. Once his visit is over, our affair will end."

"Oh." Evelyn didn't know how to respond to her sister. Her sister's denial sounded too unbelievable. Jacqueline might believe her declaration to hold some truth, but Evelyn thought differently. She glanced at Charlie and knew her twin felt the same. Charlie gave her a slight nod to confirm Evelyn's thoughts.

"Rubbish," Abigail declared. All heads swiveled toward Abigail at her defiant tone. She stood with her hands on her hips. "You hold the same starry-eyed expressions your sisters and Gemma held during their scandalous courtships. Your need to fool yourself is pure rubbish. Why hold yourself back from loving Lord Kincaid? The man dotes on your every word. Do not think I have ignored the rumors of your stolen kisses or the longing glances passed between you two." She looked around the room. "How have all of you been so blind?" Abigail's scoff finished her speech.

Charlie laughed. "My, my. Abigail has herself in a tiff. One must wonder why?"

"Not why, but whom. Am I correct, Abigail?" Gemma asked.

Abigail shook her head, refusing to discuss what troubled her. The rest of the ladies granted Abigail her privacy and didn't question her further. Everyone knew the source of her agitation. Their cousin Lucas. His behavior toward Abigail of late was atrocious. For now, they needed to focus on Jacqueline's happiness. After the holidays, Abigail planned to venture farther north and take a position as a governess. If Colebourne allowed her to leave sooner, she would. However, she wished to spend one last Christmas with her family before she started her new life.

Abigail softened her tone. "Do you care for Lord Kincaid?"

Jacqueline wanted to pour her heart and soul out to her family. However, in doing so, she would only commit herself to Kincaid. They would be persistent in throwing them together at every opportunity. Not that Jacqueline didn't want to enjoy stolen moments with Kincaid before he left, but only on her own terms. Not the terms dictated by her family. She must guard the feelings she held for Kincaid with her heart.

"Not in the sense of a romantic love where I cannot live without him. Our connection is purely of a more intimate nature," Jacqueline whispered the last words. Her face grew warmer at the lie.

Each lady nodded with a conniving smile lighting her face. Jacqueline groaned to herself. She hadn't fooled them for one second. However, she refused to budge about her feelings for Kincaid. Let them believe what they wished. They would anyhow.

"If those are your true feelings for Lord Kincaid, then we believe you. However, I feel you should end your affair immediately before you suffer from any consequences that you cannot undo," Evelyn offered.

Jacqueline nodded. "You are correct. Our affair has reached its time to end, and I will express my wishes to him today."

"It is for the best," Evelyn comforted her.

The rest of the ladies murmured their agreement. Jacqueline pasted a false smile on her lips and questioned their presence again. "May I ask why you have gathered yourselves here? I thought we were to meet in Evelyn's bedchamber this morning."

Gemma offered Jacqueline a sheepish expression. "Our husbands overindulged last night, and none of us can host morning breakfast with the Worthington sisters. Since Abigail's room is too small, we hoped you could host. When we came to ask your permission, we found your bedroom empty, and Polly said she could not find you anywhere."

Jacqueline's eyes widened. "Oh, no."

Charlie smirked. "Exactly."

Everyone knew Polly's inability not to gossip. They all adored her, but she had the worst habit of whispering their secrets to the other servants. Never out of malice, but more along the lines of sharing the adventures she imagined them to be on.

"Do not fret. I informed her you fell asleep on my divan because we stayed awake into the early hours talking," Abigail reassured her.

"Thank you."

"Now, do you understand why you must put an end to your affair with Lord Kincaid?" Evelyn asked.

"Oh, are you discussing Lord Kincaid? I must join in." Lady Noel spoke from the doorway.

The Worthington sisters walked into the room, followed by Polly and two footmen. The maid directed the servants on where to set the trays of hot chocolate and pastries. Polly rushed the servants away once they'd performed their duties. Since Jacqueline was the hostess for the morning, she rose from the bed and passed around the hot chocolate. Each lady helped herself to the breakfast fare and settled around to discuss the gentleman of the hour, much to Jacqueline's discontent.

"I could not believe my luck when Lady Forrester paired us together for charades," Noel gushed.

"Yes, you seemed to enjoy yourself most immensely during the game," Evelyn commented, glancing toward her sister. She felt torn between Jacqueline's heartache and her sister-in-law's happiness at having the viscount's attention for a brief spell.

"Oh, I did. And I could hardly believe the viscount held such a wicked sense of humor." Noel took a sip of her drink.

"You do not say. We held no clue either. Were you aware of his wickedness, Jacqueline?" Charlie asked with a devious grin.

Jacqueline choked on her scone. After clearing her throat, she glared at her sister. "How would I know of Lord Kincaid's character? I barely know the viscount."

"Yes, barely," Abigail muttered under her breath, low enough that only Jacqueline heard.

"But is he not Lord Gray's friend? I heard he had visited the estate many times in his youth. Why, he even told me a story of how he and Lord Gray used to sneak out late at night when they were younger to steal into the local tavern, but the duke caught them," Noel rattled on.

"Yes, well… That is…" Jacqueline stumbled over her words.

"What Jacqueline is attempting to explain is that when Lucas's friends visited, they kept to themselves, especially when they got into trouble. We would only share their company at meals, not enough time to become acquainted with them on a personal level," Evelyn explained.

"That makes perfect sense. It was no different with our brothers. Even though I cannot imagine Lord Kincaid as a wild youth. He is always so serious," Eden remarked.

"A regular bore." Charlie yawned. "However, I noticed a change in his behavior myself last night. What has captured my attention and made me most curious is what he whispered in your ear during charades." Charlie's eyes twinkled with mischief.

Noel, oblivious to Charlie's questioning and the other ladies' groans, answered with sincerity. "I told him about my love of charades, and he flattered me with his opinion on my skill in the game. He may appear all prim and proper the way he follows the rules and how everyone thinks him a bore, but he is most…"

"Divine," everyone said at once and then erupted into laughter.

Everyone except for Jacqueline. Mind you, she held the same opinion, but she refused to allow his finer attributes to sway her into falling for his charms. Her body may not stand a chance at resisting him, but her heart must keep a hold of her independence. If she allowed herself to form an attachment, it would only cause her more heartache when she lost him. Her family was correct, she must end their affair. However, she wouldn't put an end to their secret trysts today. She would wait until after the hunt when he left for his estate. Then, before they traveled to Scotland, she would post a letter to him, ending their relationship. In the meantime, she would make more memories to cherish. It seemed like the perfect ending to their affair.

However, the circumstances of their time together would soon surface, causing a different ending, or perhaps a new beginning, to their affair.

Chapter Eight

Kincaid waited for Ralston to join him at the stables. Ralston wanted to check on Gemma before they took their ride. The marquess remained smitten with his new bride and pampered her in her delicate condition. Kincaid envied the bloke. He'd learned of their scandalous courtship through Jacqueline. She'd scoffed at their love at first sight sentiments when she told him about them. However, Kincaid had heard Jacqueline's own envy seeping from the gossip of their love affair.

He leaned against the fence while he waited, glancing toward the manor, hoping to catch a glimpse of Jacqueline. He had yet to see her since she left his bedchamber this morning. When she snuck away, he had stepped out into the hallway, ready to cause a distraction if he needed to. But there had been no need. The corridor had remained empty. He had returned inside and donned his clothing for the day. Before he descended the staircase, he heard laughter spilling from Jacqueline's bedroom. A smile drifted across his face as he pictured Jacqueline surrounded by her family and friends. He wondered how she explained away her ravished appearance.

With a jaunt to his step, he continued down the stairs and into breakfast. The room held an eerie quietness with the other gentlemen reviving themselves with coffee from their late-night indulgence. Colebourne, Lord Forrester, and Lady Forrester were absent, having dined earlier. He ate his breakfast in silence, but his pleasure of how he spent his evening remained plastered on his face. After Ralston had regained his composure, they scheduled a time to meet later in the day.

Now he waited with patience past the time they'd agreed upon. In the meantime, he thought of the key points he wished to convince Ralston to agree to his business venture. Once his chance with the duke fell through, Gray had convinced him to discuss his plan with Ralston, considering how perfectly it would align with Ralston and Worth's own business. Guilt consumed Gray for keeping Kincaid drinking and playing cards late into the night and thus causing him to miss his appointment with Colebourne. Kincaid assured him that the fault lay with him and no other. Over the years, Kincaid had learned to take responsibility for his own mistakes. At one time, he would lay the blame on others, but no longer.

He needed to make a good impression on Ralston. If he achieved his goal, then he could present to Colebourne his ability to support Jacqueline with the comforts of life her station provided her at present. Also, it would allow him to redeem himself with the duke from his actions in the past. In his youth, he'd made the poor judgement of letting his cock lead him down a path of destruction. The duke's guidance had saved him from destroying his future. Since that fateful night, Kincaid had changed his character and walked a different path in life. Then the path veered when he allowed an golden-haired beauty to seduce him with her innocence.

"Kincaid. I hope you do not mind, but I have invited Worth to join our discussion. Gray boasted of your idea, and I feel it has the potential to coincide with our business," Ralston said when he finally appeared.

Kincaid nodded a greeting to the gentlemen. "Not at all."

"Excellent. Shall we ride to the village for lunch?"

Kincaid and Worth agreed with Ralston, and they settled onto their horses and set off at a leisurely pace. Throughout the ride, Kincaid gave a brief introduction about his business idea and answered their questions along the way. Once they reached the village, they continued their conversation at the tavern. They ordered lunch and resumed the discussion while they ate.

Ralston cut into his meat. "I admire your concept."

"It is brilliant. If you decide to invest, this will tie in nicely with our business," Worth added.

"My thoughts exactly."

Kincaid took a drink of his ale. "I must admit, I never thought of how closely it would benefit your company until Gray brought it to my attention. The aim behind my idea was to find placement for the displaced soldiers. I believe a position in my company will boost their pride by placing them in a stable environment so they can provide for their families."

"That makes your idea commendable to support," Ralston complimented.

Kincaid tried to keep his excitement contained at Ralston's comment since it sounded like Ralston had agreed to invest in Kincaid's security firm. However, Ralston's next question swiftly dashed away Kincaid's hopes.

"May I ask why Colebourne turned down your offer?"

Ralston winced, uncomfortable about having to ask the question. But Gemma wanted to know what Kincaid's intentions were for Jacqueline. She feared her cousin indulged in an affair that would ruin her reputation, not to mention her heart, if it ever came to light. Ralston couldn't blame Kincaid for his actions because he had fallen for a Holbrooke lady. The Holbrooke ladies held the mystic power of luring gentlemen under their spells. Kincaid had become the latest victim. Nevertheless, he needed to learn Kincaid's intentions to reassure his wife. Her pregnancy scattered her emotions into unknown territory. One moment, she was her loving self. The next, she would burst into tears. Hopefully, her mood would calm when he shared Kincaid's answer with her.

Kincaid cleared his throat. "Because I failed to appear at our agreed upon meeting. So in return, he withdrew his support."

Kincaid hesitated to voice the other reason Colebourne held back from investing in his venture. If he mentioned Jacqueline, then he risked divulging their affair. He didn't wish to bring any scandal to her name or the relationship he attempted to secure.

Ralston quirked a brow. "And Jacqueline?"

Kincaid took another swallow of the ale, prolonging his reply. "She is a very charming lady."

Ralston belted out a laugh. Worth gave him a questioning glance, and Kincaid shifted in his chair, no doubt betraying his thoughts. "One that caught your fancy."

"Umm…" Kincaid continued to stall.

"It was not a question, but how I have observed your smitten regard toward my wife's cousin."

Kincaid growled. "What is your point?"

Worth sighed. "Now all of this makes perfect sense."

Kincaid focused on Worth. "What makes sense?"

Worth gestured to the three of them. "Why we are having this meeting. It is a result of Colebourne's manipulations."

Ralston slapped Worth on the back. "What a harsh accusation, my friend. I prefer to look upon our luck as a promising gesture of good fortune. Colebourne is a shrewd gentleman, and this is an offer of generosity from him. He does not manipulate, but only moves his play to his advantage."

Worth scoffed. "If you chose to perceive this to be the truth, then so be it."

Kincaid was confused. "How is refusing his support an advantage for any of us?"

"'Tis simple, really. I will start with Worth first. By refusing you, he knew you would seek another investor. I would even bet he dropped the idea into Gray's head to discuss this with me. Colebourne knew I would include Worth. Which in return would prompt Worth to invest some of his own funds. Am I correct?"

Worth nodded. "Yes. I want to partner in this venture."

"I still do not understand Colebourne's angle regarding Worth."

Ralston continued with his explanation. "If your business idea is successful, then Worth will profit handsomely. Therefore, Worth's success will impress his brother and in return make Evelyn happy. Which brings us to my involvement. It is Colebourne's attempt to extend an olive branch for the 'manipulations' of my courtship of Gemma."

"Courtship?" Worth interjected.

"Yes. *Courtship*," Ralston emphasized. "If I invest, then Gemma shall share her happiness with Jacqueline. Who in return will be most impressed with your achievement."

"And this helps my case with Colebourne how?" Kincaid asked.

"It will show him the strength of your determination to make your plan a success without him. Then you can win Jacqueline on your own terms, without the influence of Colebourne. He is a very conniving gent. By stepping back, he hopes that you and Jacqueline will form a union of your own accord. If you fail, then he will take matters into his own hands."

"Then, God forbid the outcome," Worth muttered.

Ralston took a drink. "Exactly."

"So he wants me to impress Jacqueline on my own. Why?"

"Because she is the wisest of all his wards. If he invests in your business, then she will think her uncle chose you as a groom because of that connection. If there is no partnership, you shall appear more appealing in her eyes. When you persuade her to become your bride, then Colebourne will have made another successful match."

Kincaid's brows drew together. "I disagree."

"Ralston is correct. You are the latest victim to fall under Colebourne's matchmaking madness debacle. I thank my lucky stars he does not consider me worthy enough for any of his wards," Worth quipped.

"Not true. You were engaged to my wife briefly under his demands," Ralston argued.

"I was only a decoy in his ploy to secure a match between you and Gemma."

Ralston nodded, smiling as he thought of his wife. "True."

"I watched Colebourne play his tricks at the house party with Sinclair and Worthington. I thought he attempted to make a match between Jacqueline and me. But I was mistaken. If so, he would continue to make it obvious," Kincaid disagreed.

Ralston smirked. "He made it more than obvious when he invited you to his house party in the spring and remains so by extending his invitation for you to stay on after Forrester and Selina's wedding. Colebourne invited each gentleman to his home to make a match for each of his wards. Over the past few months, he's made one match at a time. And now it is your turn with Jacqueline. He will save his son and Abigail for the last match."

Kincaid regarded Ralston with skepticism. Ever since his near scandal years ago, he had become used to Colebourne's manipulations, even recognizing them before the duke demanded his help in matters. But if Ralston spoke the truth, then the duke had deceived him. He replayed the past few months, drawing forth his memories from the house party and throughout the season where Colebourne or Lady Forrester had maneuvered him to spend time in Jacqueline's company. Not that he needed to be encouraged. Hell, he always tried to find Jacqueline alone so they could spend time together. Preferably alone. Kincaid kept nodding as all the pieces fell into place.

"Do you see my point?" Ralston asked.

"Yes."

"Now that we have cleared that matter, what is your decision, Ralston?" Worth demanded.

"I will invest and have papers drawn up and transfer funds into your account. Over time, as the business becomes more successful, I will give you the option to return my investment and give you full ownership rights."

"I want in on this deal too," Worth said.

Kincaid reached across the table and shook both gentlemen's hands. "Agreed. Thank you for your support. I believe we can make this a success."

Ralston raised his ale, and they clinked their mugs together. "To success and your luck in winning Lady Jacqueline's hand."

Kincaid drank to Ralston's toast. He needed all the luck he could get to convince a very stubborn lady to trust in their love. It was a challenge he would accept with pleasure. With Ralston's support, he'd climbed over another obstacle, and it gave him the reassurance he needed in his pursuit.

He leaned back with newfound confidence while they discussed the strategy of bringing his dream to light. Ralston's and Worth's enthusiasm helped to smash his doubts to ashes. With this new deal, he could present himself to Colebourne as a worthy suitor for Jacqueline. Also, his pursual now held a purpose. Soon he would no longer be a penniless peer of the ton but a successful viscount. Someone Jacqueline would be proud to call a husband. Now to convince her to become his wife.

It would be no easy feat, but he would find success with it as well.

Chapter Nine

Luncheon was an intimate affair, consisting of immediate family only. The Worthington clan joined Evelyn and Reese in a visit to Charlie and Jasper's estate. When Gemma sat at the table, she informed them that Ralston had taken a ride into the village with Lord Kincaid and Graham Worthington to eat lunch at the local tavern.

Disappointment settled over Jacqueline. She had hoped to spend some time with Griffen this afternoon. Each chair next to her sat empty with the hope he would sit in one of them. She'd promised her family she would break off their affair, but if he were to ask for her company around other people, she couldn't refuse him. Especially in front of Aunt Susanna. Her aunt had drilled into them the proper manners of accepting a gentleman's request. Jacqueline knew Griffen's request would hold improper intentions, even though Aunt Susanna would think otherwise. However, it would appear Jacqueline wouldn't see him until later. Perhaps she could convince Aunt Susanna to sit her next to Griffen during dinner.

To spend time with him, she must become devious in her own right. Jacqueline wouldn't renegade against the promises she made if Aunt Susanna threw them together at every opportunity.

Jacqueline had learned Uncle Theo had withdrawn his support for Griffen's business plan. On top of that, Aunt Susanna no longer tried to throw Griffen and her into each other's path. Jacqueline glanced down the table, her gaze darting back and forth between Uncle Theo and Aunt Susanna, looking for any suspicious behavior. She wondered about their sudden change in attitude concerning Griffen. It had to be part of the shenanigans in their matchmaking agenda.

However, Aunt Susanna only kept inserting peaceful comments in between Uncle Theo's and Ramsay's friendly bickering. Jacqueline smiled fondly, watching their banter. As much as they disagreed, they were as close as brothers.

Aunt Susanna caught her eye and shook her head toward the gentlemen, smiling her enjoyment. "They are as incorrigible as ever."

"Yes, your husband is today," Colebourne replied with a twinkle in his eye.

"I may be today. But you are every day," Ramsay quipped, then asked Jacqueline a question as she raised her cup to take a sip. "Where is your beau? I thought after his questioning of your whereabouts after he ate breakfast, he would sit by your side at luncheon."

Everyone at the table hushed, waiting for her reply. Jacqueline sat her cup down without taking a drink. "I have no beau."

Ramsay laughed. "Sorry, my dear. I thought the Kincaid fellow was courting ye."

"Kincaid and Jacqueline? Surely, you are mistaken, Ramsay?" Lucas questioned.

Ramsay crinkled his brows in thought. "No. I do not believe I am. I saw them taking a walk in the garden, and Kincaid cannot keep his gaze off our lovely Jacqueline. Quite smitten he is."

Lucas scoffed. "Nonsense."

Jacqueline bristled from his one-word reply. "And why is that, cousin?"

Lucas winced once he realized he'd offended Jacqueline. "Only because Kincaid has visited numerous times and never inquired about you. Why would he now?"

"So you imply I am unworthy of receiving a gentleman's interest?"

Lucas gulped, glancing around the table for any help. But he only encountered the interested gazes of his family. They would be no help. "No, that is not what I implied. I meant to say Kincaid is…"

Oakes cleared his throat from the doorway. "Sorry to interrupt, Your Grace. Lord Falcone has arrived."

Colebourne rose to welcome the gentleman as he strolled into the dining room. "Welcome, Lord Falcone. I am glad you accepted my invitation."

"Thank you, Your Grace. I am sorry I had to delay my arrival." He shook Colebourne's hand.

Colebourne indicated for Falcone to take a seat. "No worries. You have arrived now, and you could not have timed your arrival any better."

"Lord Gray, may I offer you my congratulations. Where is your lovely bride?" Falcone glanced around the table, looking for Selina.

Colebourne cleared his throat. "Yes, well…"

Aunt Susanna smoothed over the explanation with the finesse only she held. "There was a slight change with the groom. My son, Duncan, and Lady Selina fell in love. The duke and Lucas graciously stepped aside and gave them their support to wed. We are sorry you missed the celebration."

Lord Falcone nodded. "Please pass my best wishes on to them."

To change the topic, Aunt Susanna told Lord Falcone of the entertainments planned for the weekend. Soon, Uncle Theo and Ramsay joined in, discussing the fox hunt with Lord Falcone.

Jacqueline snickered behind her hand at Lucas's discomfort. When he glared at her, she only smirked at him until his eyes narrowed, promising revenge. Then her humor vanished to become replaced with her own anger. Only moments before Lord Falcone arrived, her cousin had insulted her. Why did he hold the opinion that Lord Kincaid would hold no interest in her? If anything, they had much in common. Their beliefs, their love of literature, their ease of discussing a mutual passion for life. Never once had they argued. That was, until the whole marital issue became a problem between them.

Not to mention the passion that swirled around them, drawing them into each other's arms. The way their lips connected and drew out each other's sighs. How, when he caressed her, his hands molded to her body. And when their bodies joined, they melded into one soul. Their love formed an unbreakable bond. A bond Jacqueline ached for now. They had parted a few hours ago, yet she longed for his embrace.

"Jacqueline?" Aunt Susanna cut through her musing.

She raised her head and noticed everyone was staring at her. "Yes?"

"Lord Falcone requested your and Abigail's company to join him for a stroll around the garden?"

Jacqueline slid her gaze toward Lord Falcone and saw a patient smile gracing his face while he waited for her answer. A warm blush spread across her cheeks. "Yes, that would be lovely."

Lord Falcone rose and walked over to Abigail, holding a hand toward her to help her rise. A low growl across the table caught Jacqueline's attention. Lucas glared at Lord Falcone holding Abigail's hand. When Abigail blushed from the lord's attention, it infuriated Lucas.

Lucas rose, but Uncle Theo stopped him. "Lucas," Colebourne hissed quietly.

But it was loud enough for his son to hear. Lucas resumed his seat, still glaring at the couple. Lord Falcone walked Abigail toward the door and returned to the table to help Jacqueline rise. Jacqueline slid her hand into the crook of his elbow while he led them over to Abigail.

"Abigail," Lucas growled.

Abigail turned her head slightly. "Have a pleasant afternoon, Lord Gray." She then directed her attention to Lord Falcone, inquiring about his ride from London.

Jacqueline stayed quiet for most of the walk throughout the garden. While Lord Falcone was a very charming companion, he wasn't Griffen. But Jacqueline noticed the attention he paid Abigail. It gave her friend's pride a boost from where Lucas had torn it down of late. Her cousin continued taking the wrong approach with Abigail. If he wasn't careful, he would lose her to another gentleman. While it might not be Lord Falcone, another suitor would give Abigail what she searched for. Until then, Jacqueline hoped Abigail enjoyed the special attention she deserved.

Jacqueline sat on a bench and watched the couple as they discussed the roses. She wondered why Uncle Theo had invited Lord Falcone to Colebourne Manor. It couldn't be for Abigail or Jacqueline. Uncle Theo wanted Abigail and Lucas to admit to their love for one another. He wanted Lucas to earn Abigail's affections. Only Lucas kept blundering every opportunity given to him. She knew in her heart that Uncle Theo meant Griffen for her. Was there a particular reason for changing his mind? Yes, Griffen held no means to support her, but he was Uncle Theo's first choice for a groom.

Jacqueline recalled, during the season, Lord Falcone would ask for her hand to dance at every ball they both attended. They even shared the dinner dance twice during the season. Did Uncle Theo encourage both men to win her affections? She wouldn't put it past her uncle. Why, he'd even attempted that trick with Sinclair and Worthington for Charlie's hand. And then again with Ralston and Graham Worthington over Gemma.

Now she was more confused than ever. She didn't want to encourage Falcone, nor did she want to marry Griffen. Jacqueline could only handle her involvement with one gentleman at the moment. She knew what she must do. She must persuade Aunt Susanna to place her at Griffen's side whenever she could.

Jacqueline rose from the bench and excused herself once she saw Gemma and Ralston striding along the path. Abigail would be in safe hands with them as chaperones. If Ralston had returned, then so had Griffen. While she wished to search for him, she needed to have her discussion with Aunt Susanna first. Then she would tempt Griffen into stealing away with her. After all, their time spent together was slipping away before she must end their relationship.

Threat or no threat from him, their time would come to an end.

Chapter Ten

Jacqueline found Aunt Susanna in the small office next to her uncle's study. Uncle Theo had converted the room into an office for Aunt Susanna to use whenever she visited. There, she would write her correspondence and take care of matters concerning the estate. She gave the home a feminine touch after years of neglect. After Aunt Olivia passed, Uncle Theo had fallen into a deep depression from his loss. The loss of his brothers and their wives brought him another five children to raise. Their arrival had seemed to lift his and Lucas's spirits. He'd asked his wife's sister to help him since he held no clue on how to relate to five girls. However, through the years, he'd formed a loving relationship with each of them.

All the girls considered Aunt Susanna their own aunt, and she embraced them in the same manner. Through the years, everyone had grown closer as they worked through their grief at losing the ones they loved. As the oldest child, Jacqueline had assumed the role of a parent when Aunt Susanna wasn't in residence. She guided the girls through hardship, dried their tears, praised them for their achievements, and gave them the love they'd lost. She never wanted a single thing from them but their happiness. However, sometimes Jacqueline needed the gentle guidance of a mother, and Aunt Susanna offered her arms whenever Jacqueline needed her. Even when she returned to her own estate, they kept in touch with weekly letters.

As much as she wanted to persuade Aunt Susanna to throw her together with Kincaid, she also needed her sage advice on the gentleman. Maybe she could help settle Jacqueline from the lingering doubts that clouded her judgement.

She knocked on the door. "May I interrupt?"

Aunt Susanna raised her head and smiled warmly. "Yes, dear. Why not close the door for privacy. It has been a while since we've had a friendly visit."

Jacqueline closed the door and took a seat on the sofa near the fireplace. Aunt Susanna joined her and waited for Jacqueline to speak. She twisted her hands in her lap, unsure how to convey her feelings without giving too much of her relationship with Kincaid away.

Aunt Susanna placed her hand over Jacqueline's. "You have something on your mind?"

Jacqueline sighed. "Yes."

Aunt Susanna patted Jacqueline's hands before pulling away. "Take your time, dear. No need to force out your troubles until you have your thoughts settled."

Jacqueline blew out a breath. "That is the problem. I cannot settle my thoughts and hoped you could offer me some insight."

"On?" Aunt Susanna prompted.

"Lord Kincaid."

"Oh."

Jacqueline closed her eyes, then opened them again to see Aunt Susanna's knowing expression. "Yes. Oh."

Aunt Susanna laughed. "Can I safely assume that Lord Kincaid is not the only one smitten?"

Jacqueline nodded. “You may assume correctly. However, Uncle Theo no longer considers him a suitable match. Then there is my wish not to wed any gentleman. I prefer to spend my life alone. I have enough family to fill the void of loneliness and companionship. But I wish to enjoy his company when he visits.”

“Only enjoyment? You hold no other feelings for Lord Kincaid?”

Jacqueline rushed her answer. “No. Nothing else.”

“Bollocks!”

Jacqueline gasped. “Aunt Susanna!”

“You heard me, missy. You speak utter nonsense with your denial. I’ve seen you in Lord Kincaid’s company. You do not fool me for a second. I have even witnessed a kiss you shared with the lord.”

Jacqueline blushed. “Yes. Well… He only…”

Aunt Susanna settled back against the cushions with a smug look. “Exactly.”

Jacqueline tilted her head back and stared at the ceiling. “What am I to do?”

“What do you wish to do?” Aunt Susanna asked softly.

Jacqueline turned her head toward her aunt. “I am too scared to act upon what I wish for.”

“And that is?”

“I want what Charlie, Evelyn, Gemma, and even what Duncan found with Selina. A husband who fills my days and nights with a love so profound it chases my fears away. A marriage like what you share with Ramsay.”

“Does Lord Kincaid qualify for that position?”

Jacqueline sighed. “Yes.”

“But?”

"But what if I lose him? What if I find myself alone once again, surrounded by heartache? I do not know if my heart can handle the pain his loss would bring," Jacqueline explained, her voice quivering.

Aunt Susanna drew Jacqueline into her arms and offered her a mother's warm embrace. "Life does not come with guarantees. As much as we wish it to, it does not. That is why it is called life. We are meant to embrace life and live each day as a grand affair. If we live in fear, then we allow fear to win. What if you do not allow yourself to love Lord Kincaid? What if you do not open your heart to new experiences? Only you can answer those questions. I believe you will live in regret for not taking a chance at a slice of happiness for yourself."

When Jacqueline didn't answer, Aunt Susanna continued. "Oh, my dear, I have watched you grow into an amazing lady. At a young age, life forced you into a motherly role. You took on a responsibility no one expected you to, but you did so with grace, making everyone proud. You deserve everything your heart desires, but no one else can make your decisions. Only you can. We can only offer our love and support."

Tears slid along Jacqueline's cheeks while she lay in her aunt's arms. Jacqueline thought over Aunt Susanna's advice. While taking the chance was tempting, she still clung to her fear. She didn't know if she could ever release the bonds and open her heart so completely.

Jacqueline wiped her tears away and pulled out of her aunt's arms. She attempted to smile. "Thank you for your advice."

"And Lord Kincaid?"

"I will consider him and his offer."

Aunt Susanna's brows drew together. "Offer?"

Jacqueline winced. She had spoken too much. Now she would have to tell Aunt Susanna of Kincaid's marriage proposal. "He asked for my hand in marriage."

"Without asking your uncle's permission first?"

"Yes."

"Mmm. And your answer was?"

Jacqueline grimaced. "No."

"Is there a reason Lord Kincaid asked so presumptuously?"

Jacqueline felt the warmth of a blush cover her face and neck. "No," she denied.

Aunt Susanna narrowed her gaze, taking in Jacqueline's blush, and knew her statement was false. While she and Theo knew Jacqueline and Kincaid stole away together for brief spells, she didn't realize it had transgressed past innocent affections. Jacqueline's reaction confirmed that she'd shared intimacies with Lord Kincaid. This changed everything Theo had planned. His attempt to make Kincaid jealous of Lord Falcone's attention toward Jacqueline would result in a scandal. How they had escaped one with the other girls was pure luck. With Theo throwing Falcone into the mix, they might never recover from the disgrace since Falcone held no clue about their matchmaking madness.

She watched Jacqueline grow more nervous and attempted to reassure her. "Very well. I will not inform your uncle of Lord Kincaid's offer. However, you must make a decision on whether to accept his proposal. And to do so, you must spend time with him. Not alone, though," she stressed.

"No, of course not. Perhaps you can sit us next to each other when you arrange the seating order and partner us for the entertainments." Jacqueline tried to insert the main reason she'd sought out Aunt Susanna.

"Yes. That is an excellent idea. Leave it to me to throw Lord Kincaid and you together without drawing your uncle's notice."

"What about Uncle Theo? He has withdrawn his support of Lord Kincaid."

"Your uncle has his reasons for his actions. But do not worry about him either. I will enlist Ramsay's help to keep your uncle occupied."

Jacqueline raised her brows. "That is a disaster waiting to happen."

Susanna laughed with glee. "But just the distraction we may need."

Jacqueline rose and bent over to kiss her aunt's cheek. "You are the best," she whispered before leaving.

Susanna's face lit with a devious smile as she watched Jacqueline leave. Over the course of the next few days, she would guide the lovely couple to a lifetime of love and happiness. She would keep this information to herself for a while. Theo didn't need to learn how far Lord Kincaid had overstepped his bounds. Not yet, anyway. By the end of the week, Lord Kincaid would prove himself worthy.

And Jacqueline would realize the destiny the universe held for her.

Chapter Eleven

Kincaid strode into the library. Gray peered out the window into the garden with a scowl on his face. He stared over his friend's shoulder to find the source of his displeasure. Walking in the garden were Abigail and Jacqueline with Lord Falcone. Kincaid growled his own displeasure at the sight.

When the two ladies laughed over a comment the lord made, Kincaid muttered, "Bloody bastard."

Gray jerked to attention and glanced over his shoulder. He nodded before scowling out the window again.

"When did he arrive?" Kincaid growled.

"During luncheon. Then he invited them for a walk in the garden. Now they are laughing gaily at his debonair charm. My father and his interfering ways." Gray pushed away from the window and slumped into a chair.

Kincaid settled into the opposite seat and drummed his fingers on the arm. His gaze kept glancing back toward the windows. He hoped to catch a glimpse of Jacqueline again, but the trio walked farther into the garden, out of sight.

Gray continued with his rant. "He invited Falcone here for Abigail. That scoundrel isn't worthy enough for her. Abigail deserves for a gentleman to treasure her, not for the treatment she would suffer from a reprobate like Falcone."

Kincaid swung his gaze back toward his friend. "Falcone is not meant for Abigail, but for Jacqueline."

"No. My father was very specific when he told me he invited a gentleman here for my wedding with the very intention of making a match for Abigail. Falcone spoke his apologies when he arrived for his delay, then preceded to congratulate my marriage," Gray argued.

Kincaid laughed but stopped when his friend snarled. "Sorry. But you are incorrect. Colebourne informed me he invited Lord Falcone here for Jacqueline."

"Why would my father confide in you?"

Kincaid sat up straighter. "Because I asked him for permission to court Jacqueline. I want to marry her."

"Then it is true?"

"What is true?" Kincaid asked.

"You are smitten with my cousin. When did this happen?"

Kincaid ran a finger behind his cravat, uncomfortable with the question. But if he wanted his friend's support, he must confess his improper behavior. Well, confess enough to pacify Gray. "Over the last three years."

Gray exploded out of his chair. "Three years!"

Kincaid rose and moved behind the chair, hoping the furniture would protect him from Gray's pounding. "Will my case help if I tell you how much I love her?"

"No," Gray growled, advancing on Kincaid. "You are no bloody different than Sinclair, Worthington, Ralston, or Forrester. Every single one of you has acted on your selfish urges. Is no lady in this household safe from the rakes of our society?"

"Do not treat our affections for the ladies we love as tawdry affairs. Just because you hold back your feelings for Abigail does not mean I intend to disregard my feelings for Jacqueline."

Gray leaned over the chair, his fists ready. "Did you ruin her?"

Kincaid took a few steps back. "You ask too personal of a question."

Gray rounded the chair. "No, I do not believe I do. You have overstepped the bounds of our friendship."

"I may have, but I do not regret any of it."

Gray swung out and clipped Kincaid on the chin. Kincaid growled and retaliated, striking Gray across the side of his head. He never intended to fight with him, but he wouldn't stand down. Kincaid risked everything by admitting his infatuation. As they circled each other, both men growled their frustrations.

"You will leave this property immediately," Gray demanded.

"Not until I have secured Jacqueline as my bride."

Gray lunged at him again, knocking them to the floor. They wrestled around, each trying to punch the other. Kincaid's coat ripped when he tried to block a jab. Before Gray could land another swing, Ralston yanked him off Kincaid.

"Stop fighting, both of you!" Gemma shrieked.

Gray shook Ralston off him and stormed toward the door. Before he reached it, Gemma stopped in front of him, holding her hands out. "You are not leaving this room until you explain yourself," Gemma ordered.

"Why do you not ask Casanova?" Gray replied with sarcasm.

Gemma laughed. "That is quite a slander toward Lord Kincaid."

Gray growled. "No, 'tis quite fitting."

Gemma smiled at Kincaid. "Does this concern Jacqueline?"

Kincaid nodded. He propped his back against the bookcase and stayed silent. It was one thing to admit his actions to Gray, but informing other members of Jacqueline's family would only force a marriage. While his greatest desire was to make Jacqueline his wife, he didn't want their marriage to occur under duress.

Gemma glanced back and forth between Lucas and Kincaid, but they both refused to appease her curiosity. She sighed. This had spiraled out of control since Jacqueline had confessed to them this morning. It went far deeper than any of them could imagine. However, each gentleman refused to discuss the matter in front of her.

"Barrett, will you be a dear and stay until they settle their disagreement? I am retiring to our bedchamber for a spell."

Ralston went to Gemma's side, concern written all over his face. "Are you unwell?"

Gemma stood on her tiptoes and brushed a kiss across his cheek. "No, my love. Only tired and needing my afternoon lay in." She lowered her voice to a whisper. "Make sure they settle their differences before you leave. Jacqueline's happiness depends upon it."

Ralston nodded, pulling his wife into a hug before releasing her. "I will try."

Gemma offered him her sweetest smile before she left. Ralston turned and narrowed his gaze at the two gentlemen. It would appear he must rescue Kincaid from destruction once again. He knew how the viscount suffered from loving a Holbrooke lady and the obstacles he had to overcome before he could win Jacqueline's hand. Kincaid needed the approval of Colebourne, Gray, and the lady herself.

Ralston extended a hand to help Kincaid to his feet, then gestured for both gentlemen to sit. Once everyone had settled, he waited patiently for either of them to speak.

When no one was forthcoming, Ralston tried to make peace. He quirked a brow at Kincaid. "I take it Gray has learned of your secret affair with Jacqueline?"

Gray growled. "You knew! Does everyone in this household know?"

Ralston brushed an imaginary piece of lint off his trousers. "I cannot speak to the depth of your family's knowledge of how much they know. Worth only knows Kincaid holds feelings for Jacqueline, and the Worthington ladies are clueless about their affection. As for the newcomer, Lord Falcone, I am sure he is unaware. Which leaves us with Colebourne and the Forresters' knowledge. From what I experienced myself under your father's matchmaking attempt, he knows everything, and since Lady Forrester is his co-conspirator, then she is aware, too."

"How could you?" Gray asked Kincaid.

"I never intended to dishonor Jacqueline."

"What are your intentions with her?"

"I have asked her repeatedly to become my bride. And she has denied each offer. However, I gave her an ultimatum. She has until after the fox hunt to accept my proposal or I will admit our affair to Colebourne."

Ralston laughed. "Do you believe that will redeem yourself with Colebourne or Jacqueline? You are clearly an amateur."

Kincaid snarled. "So we progressed from joining forces in business to having you insult me."

Ralston gestured for Kincaid to calm down. "I only state that you attempt to handle this in the wrong manner."

"You aim to help him?" Gray asked in disbelief.

"Yes. And if you were his friend, you would, too. Your father chose Kincaid for Jacqueline's groom."

"Impossible."

"Why do you not believe Ralston?" Kincaid asked. "And have you always held such a low opinion of me?"

Gray shook his head. "No. You've proven your loyalty as a friend, even though you have betrayed me by seducing my cousin. But I understand how my father operates, and he would want Jacqueline settled with someone of Falcone's caliber, not with a dissolute viscount who could not provide Jacqueline the luxury she is accustomed to."

"For one, you judge your cousin harshly. She isn't a pampered princess, and while my lack of wealth is meager, it will not remain so. Yes, we will struggle until my business venture is stable, but I will provide for her. Our relationship is more than the status of my wealth," Kincaid argued.

"I understand your value. But my father will want Jacqueline to have the same lifestyle as her sisters and cousin, one befitting the Holbrooke name. You, my friend, cannot provide those conditions."

Kincaid raked his hands through his hair. "I am well aware of my downfalls."

Ralston cleared his throat. "Gentlemen, I think you are forgetting the primary objective. Colebourne wants Kincaid for Jacqueline. His ploy is to make Kincaid prove himself. When he set about inviting us to his house party, he only did so with the intention of each gentleman marrying one of his wards. Since you are the last gentleman standing, and Jacqueline is the final lady, then it only stands to reason he wishes for you to wed each other. Like all the other matches, he entertains himself by watching your courtship and throwing out obstacles to prove how much you love one another. Listen to my opinion, these are his intentions."

"Jacqueline is not the only unwed lady in this household. Abigail remains unwed, and my father threatened to invite his choice for Abigail to my wedding. He did not state who he was. And Falcone mentioned his regret at missing my wedding when he arrived. I believe he intends Falcone for Abigail, and I will do everything in my power to stop that union from happening."

Ralston shook his head. "Falcone is nothing but a ploy in your father's matchmaking mischief. Gray, when will you see what your father and everyone else in this family wish for?"

Gray refused to answer Ralston's question because it was impossible. While he wished for a future with Abigail, they would suffer from the consequences of their union. He refused to subject Abigail to the hardship of the ton's slander. They were a vindictive lot and would make Abigail's life miserable with their vicious tongues. He'd watched their reactions over the season when she started arriving at the entertainments with the rest of the family.

While many gentlemen sought her hand for dances, pretending an interest in the duke's ward, the whispered words in the clubs spoke otherwise. None of them had an interest in her for marriage other than to warm their beds. There were many instances Kincaid had dragged him away from unleashing his fury on his peers. Now he learned his friend carried on with his cousin in the same manner.

Kincaid watched Gray struggle with his emotions. He knew his friend's reasons for not pursuing a relationship with Abigail Cason. Gray thought he protected Abigail from the harsh treatment of the ton, instead of seeing how his family and friends would protect them if he took a chance on the lady. However, from what Jacqueline had told him, Abigail was just as stubborn as Gray. Kincaid also knew he'd angered his friend by seducing Jacqueline and leading her down a path of scandal. But he would never regret his actions.

"What advice do you offer on how I should proceed with Colebourne and Jacqueline?" Kincaid asked Ralston.

"With the lady, I would suggest you tell her you have reconsidered telling Colebourne about your affair, that you understand her reluctance, and seduce her until her answer is yes," Ralston suggested.

"You are discussing *my cousin*," Lucas growled.

Ralston nodded. "My apologies."

"And Colebourne?"

"Ahh, he is a little trickier. Colebourne is a sneaky devil. You will need to instigate yourself near him whenever you can and turn his game around on him."

Gray bristled. "Now you are talking about *my father*."

Ralston smirked. "My apologies again."

Gray blew out a breath. "Fine, I will help you."

Kincaid raised a questioning brow. "You will?"

"Yes, against my better judgment." He rose and offered his hand to Kincaid. "In truth, I cannot ask for a better husband for my cousin. You both deserve happiness."

Kincaid shook Gray's hand. "Thank you."

Gray walked over to the window again and stared outside. While he offered his help, he still was wary of Falcone's arrival. Ralston argued Falcone was only a decoy, but his father wouldn't have invited the gentleman here without a reason. His father always had a purpose when he invited guests into his home. He didn't open his estate up to just anyone.

Only to those close family and friends. If the occasional visitor arrived, it was because the Duke of Colebourne needed the individual for his own reasons. And his father kept those reasons to himself.

Gray narrowed his gaze when he noticed Abigail walking alone with Lord Falcone in the garden. Where had Jacqueline disappeared to? "Excuse me, gentlemen. There is a matter I must attend to." He rushed out of the library.

"I wonder where he is off to," Kincaid mused.

Ralston tilted his head out the window. "Probably on his way to stick his foot in his mouth."

Kincaid looked out the window to see Abigail unchaperoned with Lord Falcone. He saw the reason for Gray's swift departure and felt sympathy for him. He understood Gray's tormented emotions, for he'd had the same reaction whenever Jacqueline danced with another gentleman during the season. No matter how innocent it appeared, jealousy consumed him.

"Now that Gray has left, shall you explain what Colebourne holds over you?" Ralston asked.

Kincaid tilted his head in question. "Whatever do you mean?"

Ralston smiled with patience. "I mean, what has Colebourne used against you over the past few years for you to jump to his bidding whenever he requested it of you? I only ask because at one time I stood in your very shoes."

"He helped me escape from a scandal that would have ruined my family's name. Since then, I have accomplished his tasks and bided my time until I fulfilled my end of the bargain. When he issued me the invitation to his house party in the spring, he informed me of his terms. I was to marry his ward, and it would end our agreement. Only making Jacqueline my bride would be of no hardship."

"May I ask who the scandal revolved around?"

Kincaid sighed. "None other than Lord Falcone's sister."

Ralston's eyes widened. "The Duke of Gostwicke's wife? That sister?"

Kincaid nodded.

Ralston laughed. "Oh, Colebourne is cleverer than I thought."

"Yes, he is. With Falcone's arrival, the duke has forced me in a corner to admit to the indiscretion of my past, thereby throwing another obstacle in my plan of convincing Jacqueline to believe in our love."

"Sometimes the truth is a powerful blessing for a couple. It strengthens their bond."

Kincaid regarded Ralston with skepticism. "And you have shared your past indiscretions with Lady Gemma?"

Ralston nodded. "Every worst act imaginable I might have been a part of."

Kincaid rose from the chair. "Thank you for your advice. Now if you will excuse me, I have a lady I need to *seduce*."

Ralston laughed. "Best of luck, my friend."

Kincaid needed more than luck. He needed a miracle.

Chapter Twelve

Jacqueline left Aunt Susanna's study and made her way to her bedchamber. Her late night spent in Griffen's arms had caught up with her. She hoped that, after a nap, she would gain a new perspective on how to handle Griffen and the consuming feelings he invoked in her. She longed for his arms to comfort her, but it wasn't a wise course of action. When she yawned, tiredness consumed her. Perhaps they could sneak into his bedchamber and share a few kisses before dinner. Enough to satisfy her needs before she showed her family how she kept her distance.

When she reached the landing, she heard footsteps running up the stairs. She gripped the railing and twisted to see who rushed up behind her. A very disheveled Griffen. His hair stood on end, and his face supported a bruise. The bluish coloring gave him an air of danger. His torn suit coat made clear of a scuffle. *But with whom?*

Before Jacqueline could stop herself, she reached out and gently touched his cheek. "Oh, Griffen. What happened, my love?"

Griffen stilled at her touch, savoring the loving gesture. He should enjoy her concern, but her endearment prompted him to make an ass of himself. "Ahh, I knew you loved me. Why do you continue to deny it?"

Jacqueline jerked her hand away. While Griffen voiced his opinion loudly to annoy her, her reaction at expressing an endearment troubled her more. "Hush. I only spoke out of concern, nothing more. Now explain yourself."

He smiled a cocky grin. "So you say, *my love*. Gray attacked me in your defense."

"Why?" Jacqueline asked wearily.

Griffen shrugged. "I suppose he felt the need to defend your honor."

"Why?" Jacqueline hissed. An uncomfortable foreboding overcame her.

Griffen winced. "Because I might have informed him of our affair."

Jacqueline closed her eyes and swayed at his answer. No! Her worst nightmare unfolded before her very eyes. Lucas wouldn't stay silent about this. He would make his demands clear for Uncle Theo to force her into a marriage with Griffen. A marriage she was unsure she wanted. This was a disaster.

When Jacqueline swayed, Griffen caught her before she tumbled down the stairs. He lifted her in his arms and glanced down at her pale complexion, wanting to kick himself for distressing her. He continued to her bedchamber. Thankfully, the door stood open, and he laid her on the bed. He returned to the hallway and saw they were alone. Griffen closed the door and returned to Jacqueline's side.

Her eyelids fluttered open, and the color returned to her cheeks. He breathed a sigh of relief and sat next to her on the bed, holding her hand in his. "Jacqueline," he whispered.

"Griffen."

"How are you feeling, love?"

Jacqueline drifted far away, but Griffen's calming voice lured her back to him. "Tired." She turned her head and noticed that she lay on her bed, but she didn't remember how she got there. "Why are you in my room? You must leave before someone finds you," Jacqueline murmured sleepily.

"You fainted on the staircase. I will leave once I am sure you are well. Do you want me to call for Lady Forrester or your sister?" His hand shook when he brushed the hair from her eyes.

Jacqueline becoming ill again didn't settle well with him. When she didn't answer him and instead stared at him with her sleepy eyes, he wanted to wrap her in his embrace and hold her until she recovered.

"Nonsense. I do not faint." She tried to rise, but exhaustion overtook her, and she fell back against the pillows. "I am sleepy and need to rest."

Griffen sighed. "You may not usually faint, but you did so moments ago."

Jacqueline covered her hand over her mouth, fighting a yawn. "Mmm. If you say so, Lord Kincaid. However, I beg to differ. I only ask you to stay silent and not tell a soul."

Griffen shook his head at her stubbornness. "I promise, only if you promise to rest for the afternoon."

Jacqueline's eyes drifted closed. "You have my promise, but only if you hold me for a brief spell."

Griffen's gaze darted to the door. His greatest wish was to comfort her, but he would risk her reputation if he stayed and someone caught them together. But when she murmured, "Griff," he was powerless to deny her.

"Ah, hell." He stood up and discarded his suit coat, unbuttoned his waistcoat, and unloosened his cravat.

He laid on the bed and pulled Jacqueline into his arms, where she snuggled into him. Her arm wrapped around his waist and tightened the deeper she fell into sleep, as if she feared he would leave her. She was a contradiction he wished he understood. Because if he did, he could convince her of their love and ease her fears.

Griffen lost track of how long he held Jacqueline, hoping she would awaken. His hand glided over her hair. The longer she slept, the more he worried about her illness. Within the past twenty-four hours, she had lost her stomach and then fainted. Now she slept dead to the world, never once moving while he held her. Who could he discuss her sickness with without raising too many alarms of their intimacy? Unfortunately, no one. And he'd made Jacqueline a promise not to betray her confidence. If he wanted to prove his trust, then he needed to keep her illness to himself for now.

The bell for dinner rang out through the manor. He must leave before Jacqueline's maid came to help her dress. He pulled his arm out from underneath her and eased off the bed. When Jacqueline murmured his name, Griffen stilled and looked over his shoulder to see she remained sleeping. With reluctance, he gathered his clothing, bent down to brush a kiss across her cheek, and took his leave through the secret passageway. He didn't dare take a glance over his shoulder when he left. It would only make him yearn for forbidden circumstances. At least, he made it to his bedchamber without crossing paths with anyone.

~~~~~

Jacqueline heard the mirror creak shut and opened her eyes. She was a coward for avoiding Griffen. Even after he held her with tender affection while she slept. But if she'd shown him she awakened, she would've had to stare into his concern-filled eyes. She'd seen the worry in them before she fell asleep. He wanted her to seek the advice of Aunt Susanna or the local physician for her ailments. However, there was no need to discover what ailed her. Jacqueline accepted the truth of what she kept denying.
~~~~~

Her hand drifted over her stomach and curved around the softness. While she slept in his arms, a dream of a family they'd created invaded her sleep. She dreamed of how Griffen walked a crying infant around in circles, whispering a story until the babe quieted. Then he brought the child to their bed and laid it between them. He whispered into the night about what an amazing child they'd created together and how lucky he was to have her for his wife.

When she awoke, she realized why she had gotten sick and the tiredness overcoming her at odd times. Not to mention how she'd fainted at the sight of Griffen being injured. The stress had overtaken her and landed her in his arms. All because a babe grew within her. A child created from their passion, the time where their love flourished. A love Jacqueline feared to embrace.

Her predicament would cause many to rush into a marriage. However, Jacqueline needed to overcome her fears and her need for independence. She would marry Kincaid, but it would happen on her terms, not the wishes or demands of others.

In the meantime, she would seduce the *divine* viscount into accepting her terms.

~~~~~

Jacqueline got her wish.

Aunt Susanna placed her next to Griffen during dinner. However, she also sat her next to Lord Falcone, who was an incorrigible flirt. Not only with her, but also with Abigail, who was his other dinner companion. Jacqueline arrived late to the drawing room before dinner, leaving Griffen to escort her to the dining room. But not too late to notice the tension between
~~~~~

Griffen and Falcone. Every time Falcone flirted with her, Griffen would grab her hand to remind her he sat next to her.

As if she could forget how close he was. His very scent surrounded her, conjuring forth memories of lying in his bed as he worshipped her body. When he talked, his fingers glided over hers, stroking her from the tips of her fingers to her wrists. It reminded her of how he stroked her to climax. Jacqueline shifted in her seat, clasping her thighs together. She fought against the urges of the sensations he brought forth with his exquisite caresses. His voice softened when he addressed Lady Worthington on his other side. Oh, how she longed to hear him whisper his scandalous thoughts in her ear.

Kincaid smiled at Lady Worthington as he made polite dinner conversation. He really wanted to smile wickedly at Jacqueline. He heard her whisper-soft sighs when he circled her wrist and ran his thumb across her quickened pulse. When she kept shifting in her chair, he knew he'd snared her attention. He would do anything to keep her focused on him instead of Falcone. He still didn't understand Colebourne's agenda for inviting the marquess to the hunt, other than to force Kincaid's hand. Ralston had urged him to confide in Jacqueline about his past, but he decided against it. His current status stood unfavorable, and the transgression from his past would only give Jacqueline another excuse to refuse his proposal.

Jacqueline's breath hitched when Griffen slid his hand along her thigh. Her legs parted, answering his unspoken demand. His fingers responded, brushing across her core. Kincaid didn't need to see Jacqueline's response to sense how his touch affected her. The connection between them made everyone else's presence disappear. Only the two of them existed.

Well, that was how he tried to fool himself.

"Are you unwell, Lady Jacqueline?" Lord Falcone inquired in a low voice.

A blush washed over Jacqueline. "No, Lord Falcone."

"I only ask because your meal is untouched."

Jacqueline wanted to slide out of the chair and hide underneath the table. She didn't think anyone had noticed her distraction, but she was mistaken. She swatted at Griffen's hands, pushing them away as discreetly as she could without Lord Falcone seeing. Jacqueline turned toward the marquess and lowered her lashes. "Am I too obvious?" she whispered.

Lord Falcone glanced around the table before focusing his gaze on Jacqueline. "Only to me."

Jacqueline smiled sweetly, hoping she could fool him into believing her. "I fear I overindulged during afternoon tea. I ate one too many sweets. My stomach is full, and I have no wish to offend our cook by not eating the meal."

Falcone smiled knowingly. "Ahh, I understand your dilemma."

"I hope you do not think too poorly of me."

"On the contrary, I admire your thoughtfulness toward the servants. Few would be so considerate. My admiration for you grows," Falcone complimented Jacqueline.

He may be a shameless flirt, but the marquess also breathed substance. Jacqueline had been quick to dismiss him but changed her opinion. Her smile widened. "Thank you, my lord."

Falcone swapped her plate without anyone seeing his noble move. "My pleasure, my lady. Now do not think me too discourteous, for I must finish this fine meal before me."

Jacqueline laughed softly so as not to draw attention to them. "Not only charming but gallant, too."

He winked at her. Jacqueline turned forward, picked up her glass, and took a drink. She smiled over the pleasant exchange, feeling a kindred spirit with the lord. He wasn't what he presented himself to be. While he flirted with her, she felt it was only his personality and how he conducted himself with all females. She had spent enough time with him throughout the season whenever he asked her to dance to know he had no intention of pursuing her. He only passed his time by spending company with any lady who paid him attention. Jacqueline decided Lord Falcone would make a fine friend.

She wasn't a fool. Uncle Theo had invited Lord Falcone to Colebourne Manor for a reason, one she was clueless to. She thought Falcone might be a distraction to make Lucas take notice of how Abigail would make someone else a charming wife if he didn't confront his feelings for her.

The hostility between Griffen and Falcone drew her curiosity. She didn't dare turn her head to the left because she knew the exchange she shared with Falcone had infuriated her lover. Tension rolled off him in waves. An innocent smile graced her features, so as not to draw any attention their way. Her involvement with Griffen had already spread throughout her family, and before long, her uncle would learn of their affair. Jacqueline needed to question Griffen about what he'd told Lucas because her cousin kept glaring at them throughout the meal. Except for when Falcone held Abigail's attention, then Lucas's gaze focused on them instead.

"Jacqueline." Griffen gritted her name between his teeth.

Jacqueline turned her head and gifted Griffen with the same smile she had Lord Falcone. "Yes, Lord Kincaid?"

Griffen snarled. "What did that reprobate whisper to you?"

Before Jacqueline answered him, Aunt Susanna concluded the meal. "Ladies, shall we retire to the drawing room while the gentlemen enjoy their brandy and cigars? Do not dally too long, Colebourne. I've planned card games for this evening's entertainment."

Griffen made one last attempt to grab Jacqueline's hand, but she rose too swiftly and followed the other ladies. His closest touch was to brush his hand across her skirts. Falcone smirked at his obvious failure. He wanted to swipe the smug arrogance from the marquess's face, but he must keep his distance. He didn't want to raise Falcone's wrath because Falcone would reveal the scandal from his past and ruin him.

Colebourne kept to Lady Forrester's order and the gentlemen only drank one brandy before joining the ladies in the drawing room. Kincaid found himself partnered with Lady Noel. Gray and Jacqueline's sister, Lady Sinclair, played opposite of them. He tried to switch places with Worth to partner with Jacqueline, but Lady Forrester would have none of it. So Kincaid found himself distracted by Jacqueline throughout the evening, causing him to throw the game multiple times.

They were on their last hand when Lady Noel voiced her curiosity. "Lord Kincaid, you are sporting quite the bruise. Were you involved in a scuffle?"

Kincaid cleared his throat, pretending interest in his cards. "A simple misunderstanding, 'tis all."

Lady Noel turned her head toward Gray. "Was it with Lord Gray?"

Gray laid down a card, oblivious to the turn in conversation because his attention landed across the room on Abigail. "Was what?"

"Since you also sport a bruise, I assume you and Lord Kincaid partook in a scuffle. Was it a misunderstanding?"

Charlie's eyes twinkled with enjoyment at the young lady's observation. "Yes, Lucas. What caused your misunderstanding?"

Gray's gaze narrowed on his cousin, but he turned a charming smile upon Lady Noel. "As Kincaid said, only a slight misunderstanding. One that Lord Kincaid will make amends on soon."

Lady Noel gasped. "Oh, I hope it is nothing too dire to affect your friendship."

Charlie tilted her head, observing Kincaid with a shrewd gaze. "Yes. I hope it is nothing too dire," she stressed.

Kincaid met Lady Sinclair's narrowed gaze with confidence. It would appear a silent conversation played out at the table with Lady Noel, who was oblivious to its double meaning. He understood her message, but he didn't allow her threat to affect him. Jacqueline had confided in him over the past three years about her sisters' characters, and he felt he understood them as well as his own family. Charlie, while protective, held the softest heart of all the Holbrooke sisters. Her glare was her way of protecting her older sister. On that, they could both agree.

"Nothing I do not seek redemption for, Lady Noel. With my future actions, I hope to prove my worthiness." Kincaid nodded at Charlie to let her know he'd received her threat. When the lady acknowledged him with a wink, he felt he'd won her over.

Without realizing it, Lord Falcone had moved to stand behind their table. "I would not hold much stock in what Lord Kincaid professes, Lady Noel. His past has proven likewise to my knowledge."

"Falcone," Kincaid hissed in a warning.

Falcone shrugged. "What? I only offer a warning to the young ladies of your character."

Kincaid and Gray rose from the table in defense. Gray placed his hand on Kincaid's arm. When Kincaid looked at him, Gray shook his head, silently urging him not to respond. Kincaid fought against defending himself, but he didn't want to end the pleasant evening by causing a scene. Falcone would take pleasure from forcing him into one. He shook off Gray's hand and stalked out of the room.

After her round of cards ended, Jacqueline sat with Lady Eden, discussing a trip into the village on the morrow. Eden hoped shopping would distract her from her boredom and decided a stroll through the shops would help ease her dilemma. Jacqueline agreed, hoping the excursion would help clear her mind.

While they finished making their plans, Jacqueline overheard Lady Noel questioning Griffen and Lucas over their bruised faces. Lady Eden shook her head at her sister's indecorous line of questioning. Nothing was sacred with the young miss. Jacqueline envied the young lady's easygoing nature to ask whatever rambled through her mind. While many thought her a silly debutante, she was anything but. Actually, Lady Noel was quite clever.

Griffen spoke too lowly for her to hear his reply. But when Lord Falcone taunted Griffen, she overheard the insults. Why did he imply Griffen was untrustworthy? The slander was the opposite of Griffen's character. Even before she'd set out to seduce him, he was always honest. His behavior and reputation were impeccable. Why, even her sister described him as boring and predictable, a regular old biddy. However, Griffen didn't rise to the marquess's taunts to defend himself. Griffen stormed from the drawing room, and Lord Falcone appeared smug before moving outside to the terrace.

"Excuse me, Lady Noel." Jacqueline rose and followed Griffen without waiting for Noel's reply.

She should have been discreet when leaving because, unbeknownst to her, Uncle Theo watched her follow Griffen.

However, Griffen was her only concern, not the scheming notice of a matchmaker.

Chapter Thirteen

Jacqueline scanned the rooms, looking for any sign of Kincaid. She had followed him as soon as he left, but he disappeared. She couldn't find him anywhere. Jacqueline decided she would return to her room and change into her nightwear, then wait until the house was asleep to sneak into this bedchamber.

She climbed the stairs to the first landing and heard the clank of billiard balls crashing apart. When she heard a gentleman swear, she knew she'd found Kincaid.

She leaned against the door and watched him round the billiard table and line up his shot. With elegance, he pulled the cue back and slid it between his fingers before pushing it toward his intended target. The ball slid smoothly across the felt, gliding toward the pocket and rolling in. Kincaid had yet to notice her and continued to shoot one ball after another into the pockets.

If Jacqueline didn't know any better, she'd say Kincaid was a pool swindler. She had never heard where he won any games the gentleman had partaken in. If anything, they always joked about how he was the worst billiards player imaginable.

Kincaid had stripped off his suit, waistcoat, and cravat, and the top few buttons of his shirt were undone. Jacqueline's mouth watered at the tempting sight of his bare flesh, and she wished to strike her tongue against it. Her gaze traveled down the rest of his body. His breeches emphasized his muscular thighs, leaving nothing to the imagination. But Jacqueline didn't need to imagine because she'd experienced firsthand how strong they were. Especially when her own legs entwined with his.

Jacqueline shook her scandalizing thoughts away. "You play quite an impressive game, Kincaid."

Kincaid finished his shot before glancing toward the lady who consumed his every thought. He couldn't answer her without divulging the depth of his skill. Also, he no longer understood where he stood with her. Jacqueline's moods of late changed more than the direction the wind blew. So he took a drink of his whiskey and waited for her to speak.

He watched as she strolled farther into the room. Jacqueline trailed her fingers across the felt until she reached him. Then those same fingers trailed along his arm and across his back, light as a feather as she sauntered around him and continued around the billiard table. Once she reached the opposite side, her mischievous smile widened, and he grew curious at what she found so amusing. Her mood appeared quite playful, but Kincaid remained cautious. One never knew how a Holbrooke lady's mood shifted. He knew firsthand how Jacqueline was a walking contradiction. And when a Holbrooke smiled like that, one must remain on guard.

Jacqueline wanted to laugh at Kincaid's guarded expression. She realized then how much she affected him. How her flighty moods changed the way he would treat or react to her behavior. It was at that exact moment she understood the intensity of his love.

She rolled the ivory ball toward him. "Shall we play a game?"

Kincaid cocked a brow. "Do you know how?"

Jacqueline gasped, pretending that he'd insulted her. "Not only am I a skilled player, but I would declare victory if we played a game."

"You do not say. Shall we make it interesting then?" He regretted the taunt as soon as he spoke. The last billiards game he'd played involving a lady had landed him indebted to Colebourne. Their game could end in a disaster because of the risky stakes involved. But he wanted to indulge Jacqueline's mischievous nature.

Kincaid went to the wall and chose a billiard stick for her to use. Jacqueline shook her head in refusal. "No, the blue one."

He whistled at her choice. She picked a custom-made stick. He didn't know whether to chuckle or feel intimidated. When she rubbed the chalk on the tip like a skilled player preparing to play, he realized the minx might be a worthy opponent.

Jacqueline stood with one hand on her hip and the other holding the cue. "What do you have in mind, Kincaid?"

Damn if her arrogant stance didn't arouse him. "Mmm," he murmured as he strolled toward her.

He took in her full hips swung to the side and her breasts pressed forward. They pulled tight against her dress, swelling out. As he perused her, her nipples tightened into hard buds, straining against her dress. Oh, how he wished to feast upon them. To lift her onto the table and show her exactly what he had in mind.

"Kincaid?" Jacqueline tried to get his attention, but when his gaze remained focused on her breasts, she knew where his thoughts wandered. It would appear the viscount suffered from the same affliction. Jacqueline turned toward the table, breaking the spell she wrapped around him.

He cleared his throat and reached for the bottle of whiskey, pouring himself another hefty shot. "If I win, then you must meet me tomorrow night for a midnight stroll through the gardens." He wished to tempt her with an elaborate tryst but didn't want to ruin the mood of the atmosphere.

"And if I win?"

Kincaid spread out his arms. "Whatever your heart desires."

Jacqueline mused over her choices. What she desired was for Kincaid to sweep her off her feet and ravish her. And what her heart most desired, she struggled to confess. That fear left her to continue with a bet to keep with their light amusement. "If I'm the winner, then you must accompany me and the Worthington sisters into the village tomorrow while we visit the shops."

Kincaid groaned at the bet, but at least he would spend time in her company.

"And," Jacqueline continued with the details of her bet, "every time Lady Noel makes a purchase, you must offer to carry them." Jacqueline giggled.

Kincaid rolled his eyes toward the ceiling at the absurdity of the bet. If he agreed, then she would have him portraying a besotted gentleman who hoped to gain a lady's affection, which would only encourage the young miss's infatuation. Oh, he hadn't been blind to it. It was the very reason he tried to avoid Lady Noel. But he would agree because it caused Jacqueline to light up with pleasure.

He stepped forward and stuck out his hand. "I agree to your preposterous terms."

Jacqueline slid her hand into his to shake, but instead of releasing her, he drew her close. Kincaid bent his head to whisper in her ear, "A bet on this level will only become valid with a kiss."

When his lips captured hers, Jacqueline sighed into his kiss. The fierce pull of his mouth drowned her senses, drawing her deeper into the desires swirling around them. She moaned when his kiss demanded for her to submit to what his heart desired—her.

Jacqueline hovered on the edge, ready to fall into his arms, but pulled back instead. She reluctantly withdrew her lips from his, patted his chest, and stepped back. "Shall we play?"

Kincaid watched the nervous flutter of Jacqueline's hands when she prepared the table for their game. The kiss they'd shared affected her as deeply as it affected him. Perhaps even more so. The dynamics of their relationship had shifted this evening.

"Ladies first."

Jacqueline smirked. "Your first mistake, Lord Kincaid."

Kincaid threw his head back and laughed. It appeared their kiss hadn't caused her confidence to wither. If anything, it only reinforced it.

His stare never broke from her as she prepared her first shot. She wiggled her hips, lined up the cue ball, and pulled back. As the stick slid effortlessly between her fingers and hit the ball, he realized Jacqueline was no amateur player. The cue ball connected with a powerful force, sending the ivory ball to connect with the red ball. They both made their way into the pockets, showing proof of her skill.

His astonished gaze met her smug smile, and he realized he could show no mercy on his turn. "Nice start," he complimented her, and she beamed at his praise.

The game became another extension of a game in its own right. On each player's turn, the other player caused a distraction. At first, it was flirtatious comments, then it progressed into soft touches when they passed the cue back and forth. Each time, it grew into more sensuous caresses. Jacqueline found her concentration slipping further out of her control. Who knew a simple billiards game would turn into an erotic seduction.

Kincaid had rolled his sleeves up his arms and leaned on the table with his hands resting on either side of the target she needed to hit. His heavy gaze reached her, softly teasing. His fingers twirled a figure eight around the ball, heightening her desires. They both had only one more shot remaining. It was her turn, and she only needed to score a point. But she had missed making one on her last turn.

Jacqueline's resistance melted under his gaze. The air sizzled with their resistance, begging for them to stop their denial. However, it only pushed him to continue the torture. "Usually in these circumstances, the players would make an additional bet to raise the stakes higher."

Jacqueline bit her bottom lip, tempted to fall for his intimidation. "What kind of bet?"

Kincaid grinned wickedly. "One that would benefit both of us."

Her teeth scraped across her bottom lip, then her tongue slid out to soothe the bite. "What are the additional terms?"

Kincaid groaned at her wanton display of temptation. Jacqueline knew her actions would tempt him. She had hoped to distract him, but she only fueled the desire burning in his gaze. It completely backfired on her when he grabbed the billiard stick and rounded the table. With each step, she inched backward until she hit the wall. Kincaid rested the cue against the table before he bracketed his arms on either side of her.

"They are most wicked," Kincaid whispered before he kissed a path along her neck. Jacqueline closed her eyes at the wondrous sensation, her body burning for more. He paused when he reached her lips, his warm breath teasing her with anticipation. "Do you agree?"

Jacqueline drew her eyes open and stared into his devilish gaze. "Will you at least inform me of what I am agreeing to?"

Kincaid stroked his tongue across her lips, teasing them open before he pulled away. Jacqueline groaned her disappointment. He kissed his way over to her ear and whispered the most scandalous offer he could make.

Jacqueline's heart raced as he described the sensuous pleasure the winner would receive. Whatever the outcome, they would both declare victory.

"If you score a point, then I will fall at your feet and worship you with my mouth. I will draw forth your pleasure with one stroke of my tongue after another, drawing your passion to the brink of exploding. Then I will build the pressure higher and higher until you let yourself fly under my touch." He drew her earlobe in between his teeth and tugged, shooting sparks of desire through her soul.

Jacqueline gasped at the sensation. "And if you should win?"

"Well, you would return the favor in the same manner. Your warm mouth wrapped around my cock while your wicked tongue teased its sweet torment. I want to gaze upon you as you slowly slide my cock between your lips, drawing out the pleasure until I beg for release."

Jacqueline's breath caught at the scene he described. It didn't matter who won. His terms only guaranteed the pleasure they would find from the scandalous bet. She turned her head and captured his lips. She answered his terms by stroking her tongue across his lips and stealing inside to skim across his. He darted his tongue around, causing her to chase it until they entwined and their kiss merged their lips closer, each drawing the breath of the other.

Kincaid growled at her answer, pulling her into his arms. His hands raked through her hair, tumbling it down around her. The sexual tension he'd endured during their billiards game wanted to break free. His need only built the more she controlled their kiss. He hungered to spread her before him and satisfy the passion consuming him.

Jacqueline pulled her lips away before they crossed the line their lovemaking usually took. They risked too much by being alone where anyone could come upon them. Her next words shocked her as much as they did Griffen, but when one ached as she did, one would mutter anything.

"I will find much pleasure from your lips when I win."

Kincaid's eyes widened at her wanton words. But the pink spreading across her cheeks, down her neck, and across her chest endeared her to him. While trying to be a sultry temptress, she still exuded a sweet innocence. That was one of the million reasons why he loved her.

Smirking, he stepped back from her and held out his arm. "We shall see."

Jacqueline stepped toward the table, grabbed the billiard stick, and tried to concentrate on her shot. But the heady scent of Kincaid's cologne overpowered her senses. It heightened the promise of the bet. When she took her shot, the stick slipped sideways, and instead of hitting the ball, she struck thin air.

"Tsk. Tsk."

How had she missed the shot? She had taken more difficult hits before and always made them. However, in her defense, a divine viscount had never been a distraction. She handed him the cue graciously in a show of fair play. After all, he must score a point to declare himself the victor.

Kincaid smirked at his chance to win. He took the stick from Jacqueline, but not before she allowed her fingers to brush across his when she released it. He tried to concentrate, but the lingering sensation of her touch enflamed his senses. So much that when he took his shot, he hit the ball with such force it flew off the table and rolled across the floor to land at Jacqueline's feet.

Jacqueline picked up the ball and laughed. "Tsk, tsk."

Now Jacqueline was the one to smirk. He gave her another chance. Perhaps he could use this to this advantage. Plus, it gave him an excuse to hold her in his arms again. “May I offer some advice?”

Jacqueline smiled seductively. “Please do.”

Kincaid circled her, trapping her against the billiard table. He bent them to line up the shot with his hand wrapped over hers. His other hand lingered on her breasts, cupping their firmness as his fingers brushed back and forth across her nipples. “You need to position the stick at an angle when taking a shot like this, compared to how I angle my tongue against your—”

Before Kincaid finished his thought, her sisters interrupted them. “Jacqueline! What is the explanation for this blatant display of seduction? It is highly inappropriate, not to mention most improper,” Evelyn carried on.

“Do not forget truly scandalous,” Charlie agreed.

Jacqueline untangled herself from Kincaid and smoothed out her dress. “Lord Kincaid was only showing me the best way to take my shot.”

“You promised,” Evelyn protested, throwing her hands in the air.

Jacqueline sighed in disappointment. They wouldn’t get to finish their game because of her meddling sisters. “Thank you for the game, Lord Kincaid.”

Kincaid bowed. “It was my pleasure, Lady Jacqueline.”

Jacqueline smiled and winked at him, signaling her acceptance of continuing the seduction later this evening. He gave her the slightest nod, unnoticeable to her sisters, of his willing inclination. Then she left with Evelyn on her heels as she reprimanded Jacqueline all the way to her bedchamber.

“Jacqueline, you made us a promise to break ties with Lord Kincaid.”

Jacqueline smiled patiently at her sister. "Sometimes promises are meant to break."

Evelyn frowned. "That is no reason for your behavior. What if someone else came upon you alone with Lord Kincaid?"

Jacqueline gathered Evelyn's hands. "But no one did. Circumstances have changed concerning Lord Kincaid. I cannot divulge why. I only ask for you to trust me. Can you do that?"

Evelyn had no other choice. She would do anything her sister asked. Not long ago, Evelyn had found herself in a similar situation with Reese. Jacqueline had offered her unwavering support, and it was only right for Evelyn to offer the same. Her sister deserved happiness more than any of them. She had devoted her life to them when their parents had lost their lives, always sacrificing her happiness so each of them could have it instead. Not that Jacqueline lived an unhappy existence. Only, she placed everyone's needs before her own.

Evelyn squeezed Jacqueline's hands. "Yes, I can."

Jacqueline hugged Evelyn. "Thank you."

The evening had taken a pivotal turn for Jacqueline with Kincaid. She couldn't pinpoint the exact moment when her universe had clicked with him, but it had. Over the past few months, her emotions had grown with him, yet she always kept him at a distance, too afraid to leap into his arms. But when she followed him after he stormed from the drawing room, her only objective had been to ease his troubled soul. Their game of billiards proved there was more to their relationship than sizzling attraction.

They shared an unbreakable connection of friendship and lovers. While he distracted her from asking questions that she sought him out for, she soothed his bruised ego and comforted him. Sometimes, just being there for a loved one was enough to calm the person. Jacqueline hoped she offered Griffen that comfort. Because she no longer wanted to deny what they shared.

She loved Griffen Kincaid.

Chapter Fourteen

Kincaid waited for Charlie Sinclair to voice her objections. However, she never did. Instead, she stood with her arms crossed against her chest with her foot tapping a steady rhythm, and she tilted her head to the side as she regarded him. He grew impatient, wanting to learn what Jacqueline had promised her sisters that she hadn't followed through with. But he waited like a gentleman for her to speak, instead of growling his question like a neanderthal.

"I underestimated you, Lord Kincaid."

He arched a brow. "How so?"

"I took you for one of those proper gents with a pole stuck up his arse. But you have proven to be the complete opposite. Who knew the uptight viscount had a scandalous streak he kept hidden?" Charlie laughed at her own humor.

Kincaid had grown used to Charlie's brash behavior since he'd taken an interest in Jacqueline. The depth of her love for her sisters always brought out her protective mother cub instinct when she defended them. He'd learned his mistake the hard way when he voiced his dislike for Charlie's vindictive attitude toward Selina Pemberton. Even though they shared a friendship now, their cruelty had left casualties at one time. On more than one occasion, Charlie had overstepped with her revenge.

Jacqueline had closed off her bedchamber to him for a spell until he listened to her. She had explained the dynamics of her sisters, Gemma Holbrooke, and Abigail Cason, helping him understand their character and behavior. He now understood their personality traits and had come to care for them because of Jacqueline. While the lady before him had matured since her marriage to Jasper Sinclair, her true nature still shined through.

He smiled his amusement at her. "One must never judge a book by its cover, Lady Sinclair. Because hidden in the depths is a mystery ready to be discovered."

Charlie grew confused at the viscount's nonchalant manner. He didn't even show his dislike at her bold declaration of his character. "And what is your mystery, Lord Kincaid?"

"Ahh, one must never give away what makes them unique."

Charlie started nodding, finally understanding what attracted her sister to Kincaid. While she held skepticism about their relationship and not understanding her sister's fascination with the lord, she now saw the very reason Jacqueline had fallen for the viscount. He offered Jacqueline the stability she had lost long ago. Not only security, but he also made her sister smile and enjoy life again. How were they blind not to notice that Jacqueline had fallen in love?

"You are correct, my lord. One must never divulge their secrets or those of others." She winked at him before sauntering away.

Kincaid watched Charlie leave and realized she'd given him her approval of his conquest to win Jacqueline's heart. He laughed over her quirky acceptance and the relief of another obstacle removed from his pursuit to win the lovely lady who had captured his heart. However, he never learned what Jacqueline promised, but he assumed it revolved around him. Since he'd won Charlie's approval, the rest of her family would give their blessings soon.

Now he only needed to win the lady's heart.

~~~~~

After the card game, Ralston and Worth followed Falcone out onto the terrace. They found him leaning against the balustrade, smoking a cigar. His arrival already showed signs of disruption. Falcone's assignment was to locate Lady Langdale, not to visit the Colebourne estate and flirt with Lady Jacqueline and Miss Cason. But he was flirting and with a nonchalance that irritated Kincaid and Gray.

"What are you doing here?" Worth hissed.

Ralston laid his hand on Worth's sleeve to calm him. "Worth, I will handle this. We thought you'd followed Lady Langdale to the continent."

Falcone shrugged. "I lost her."

"Then find her," Worth gritted out between his teeth.

"I will resume my duties after I fulfill my obligation to Colebourne." Falcone took a puff of the cigar.

"And what is your obligation?" Ralston asked.

"The kind where my refusal will not bear well with the duke," Falcone explained.

"Not you too? Who does the duke not have performing his bidding?" Worth asked with sarcasm.

"Obviously not you," Falcone muttered.

"What happened with Lady Langdale?" Ralston tried to redirect the conversation. It was pointless to argue over Falcone's arrival because Colebourne held the cards concerning the marquess's actions. Not so long
~~~~~

ago, the duke had held control over Ralston's every move. While no more, he understood the burden the marquess suffered.

"She kept a low appearance in Paris, not drawing attention upon herself. Then she hired a companion, a plain miss, who wore the drabbest of dresses. A most uncommonly wench," Falcone explained.

"Did you attempt to make contact with the companion?" Worth inquired.

"I tried, but she slipped through my grasp. The following day, they disappeared. I searched everywhere and questioned anyone who met them. But it was like they never existed. One of my contacts is looking into some leads over in France. When Colebourne dismisses me, I will return to the continent to find her. Then we shall seek our justice against Lady Langdale."

Ralston nodded his acceptance, but Falcone's answer didn't satisfy Worth. He grew impatient to return to London himself, to delve into where she might have disappeared to. But he had promised his family he would stay until after the fox hunt. Lady Langdale had wreaked havoc on many lives, and the more the ton realized her deception, the higher the price for her capture grew each day. He wanted their agency to deliver her to the authorities, and the longer Falcone remained at Colebourne Manor, the deeper she would take cover in her underground hideaways.

"Now if you gentlemen will excuse me, I want to wish Miss Cason a pleasant evening." Falcone strode away without waiting for their reply.

Worth glanced at Ralston. "Can we trust him?"

"We must. He is our only hope," Ralston muttered.

~~~~~
~~~~~

Gray entered his father's study, ready to voice his displeasure at Lord Falcone's arrival. However, he paused over the threshold, drawing back his fury, wanting to discuss this issue calmly. Over the past few months, his father had found pleasure in antagonizing him. If he stated his demand for Falcone to stay away from Abigail, his father would make it a priority to place them together at every opportunity. No. He refused to give his father any reason to subject Abigail to the scoundrel any more than necessary.

As usual, his aunt and uncle shared a nightcap with his father. Perhaps it was just as well they were present. Aunt Susanna would keep the conversation calm while Ramsay would distract his father. As he watched them interact, he felt the familiar pang of loss. Aunt Susanna resembled his mother, not only in her appearance but also in her caring nature. Losing his mother had left an unbearable ache that he and his father suffered greatly from. But at least his father never pushed him away to deal with his loss; instead, he'd kept their bond strong over the years. His father always supported his choices and took his advice on their holdings.

The only matter they crossed swords over was Abigail Cason. Every gentleman his father introduced her to wasn't worthy enough. No, she deserved so much more. And Lord Falcone, like all the other gentlemen, wasn't a wise choice. He planned to state his case once again. Gray only hoped his father would listen.

He sauntered farther into the study. "Good evening. I hope I am not interrupting."

Aunt Susanna beamed at him. "Of course you are not. Have a seat and visit with us. Unless you want to talk to your father alone, then Ramsay and I shall say good night and retire to our room?"

Gray settled into an armchair. "No. Your company is a pleasant enjoyment to end the evening with."

"Watch it, boy, ye are speaking the same shite as ye father," Ramsay teased.

Colebourne threw his hands in the air. "Not only do you insult me, but now my offspring. And to think I gifted you with the lovely Lady Selina for a daughter-in-law."

Ramsay scoffed. "Gifted? Me son won the heart of that fair maiden. But are ye not one to rub the salt in the open wound of ye own offspring? Look at the boy, he still bleeds with heartache."

Gray shook his head at their mischief. When the two of them traded barbs, they showed no soul any mercy. Apparently, he was the amusement this evening. Not that he minded. He felt extreme happiness for his cousin Duncan and Selina. They were one of the lucky ones who had trusted in their love to help guide them through the troubles of the scandal their marriage caused. Meanwhile, he remained a coward for not taking the same chance with Abigail. He refused to acknowledge his affection for the lady. One might say he deserved the misery from watching one gentleman after another court Abigail since he refused to do the same.

"Gentlemen, your behavior is unfair to Lucas. Now, Lucas, how are you enjoying the guests who have remained for the hunt?"

Gray smiled at his aunt. "They are a pleasant diversion. I have enjoyed getting to know the Worthingtons better. I've never spent much time with his family through my years of friendship with Reese. They are very pleasant and at times a handful."

Aunt Susanna laughed. "Yes, the youngest one, Maggie, is quite spirited. They will have a devil of a time with her when she comes of age. And your friend, Lord Kincaid?"

Gray grimaced. "Fine."

Colebourne chuckled. "Fine? The bruises both of you boys are sporting speak otherwise."

"The matter is of no concern to you."

Colebourne narrowed his gaze. "Mmm. I think differently, but for now, I will allow it to settle, and I will address it a later time."

Gray shrugged. "You always do." Gray found it hard to keep his hostility in check. His father's arrogance lately had provoked him to resist his authority.

Colebourne sighed. His son remained stubborn, and try as hard as Colebourne might to push him into action, Lucas only dug in his heels and refused to budge. Susanna kept urging him to try another approach with Lucas, but it didn't matter because Lucas refused what was within his grasp because of his strict moral code that society demanded he follow. He thought if he refused Abigail, then she would never get hurt by others. In truth, she hurt from his rejection alone. Time slipped away from convincing Lucas how wrong he was.

They would travel to Scotland for the winter holiday. Then he must fulfill his bargain with Abigail. Colebourne had pleaded with her to stay and spend the holidays with the family, and if she did, then he would give his blessing for her to become a governess. A position she might have been born to, but one she was far superior to. But he'd watched her heartache during the season and blamed himself. In his attempt to keep her near, she suffered heartache from Lucas's indifference. Colebourne had hoped his son would wake up and see the treasure before him. He realized he needed to let her find the happiness she deserved.

But it wouldn't stop him from attempting to bring them together until then. "Abigail looked lovely this evening."

"She always looks lovely," Gray muttered.

"Yes. She is quite the beauty. Falcone must have thought so, too. I saw him making plans with her for tomorrow," Ramsay baited him, shooting Colebourne a wink.

Susanna frowned at her husband and shook her head for him to stop. She tried to change the subject. "I hope the weather cooperates for the hunt on Saturday."

Gray sat forward in his chair. "What plans?"

"A walk to the village," Ramsay answered.

Gray scowled, his patient attitude evaporating at the mention of Lord Falcone spending any time with Abigail. "Lord Falcone is a poor choice for Abigail. He would make her a miserable husband."

Colebourne arched his brow. "Who said Lord Falcone is for Abigail? Perhaps I invited him for your cousin."

Gray scoffed. "You already secretly made a match between Jacqueline and Kincaid."

"Is that the reason for your fisticuffs?"

Gray pinched his lips, refusing to answer. He still wasn't thrilled about how his friend had betrayed him, but it was his battle to work through. He wouldn't give his father any more ammunition against Kincaid. After watching Jacqueline all evening, Gray saw how she loved his friend, and he wouldn't steal her happiness away. In time, he would forgive Kincaid for seducing his cousin. Hell, he'd forgiven Worthington. He might as well not hold a grudge against Kincaid.

No. In fact, he would help his mate along.

He rose, deciding against confronting his father about Falcone. Instead, he would seek redemption for his friend in his father's eyes. Gray decided to throw them together and tag along to make sure they made amends. After Jacqueline and Kincaid's wedding, he would resume his task of keeping any suitors away from Abigail.

"I stopped by to ask if you and Ramsay want to go fishing Friday morning?" Gray asked.

"Why do we not go tomorrow?" his father threw back at him

"I promised to visit the tenants and deliver cookies for Selina. It was a condition to apologize for running away before our wedding."

Ramsay laughed. "The lass is devious. Are we lucky or what, my love?"

Susanna looked adoringly at her husband. "That we are, my dear."

Gray smiled at them, finding joy at the love they shared, even wishing it for himself. He turned toward his father, waiting.

"Friday it is. What do you say, Ramsay, get in one more chance before you leave?"

"Sounds good to me. Perhaps ye might even catch one this time." Ramsay snickered.

"I might be able to if you do not scare away the fish with your Scottish yapping."

"It is better than ye English chattering."

Their bantering never grew old, no matter the insult. He wouldn't mention Kincaid, but he would make sure his friend joined them. His father wasn't the only one who could play matchmaker in this family. He might have told a slight fib about his plans for tomorrow, but Selina would forgive him for using her if she knew the reason. Perhaps he would take a slight detour and deliver those cookies as a sign of his redemption. After all, he didn't want his arrival in the village to appear as if he followed Abigail and Lord Falcone. No, it was best if he caught them unaware.

Chapter Fifteen

Kincaid trudged behind the ladies, juggling the packages he held. Their laughter floated behind them as he followed them like a besotted fool. Yet, with each smile Jacqueline gifted him, he didn't care how anyone perceived him. Because he was a besotted fool. Beyond smitten. His gaze locked on Jacqueline, and he silently begged for her to turn around so he could glimpse her smile again.

However, most would think Lady Noel was the lady of his unwavering attention since it was her packages he carried. At each shop, he would stand waiting and offer to carry the items she purchased. When he first offered, she had shown her delight at receiving his attention. He'd smiled when he overheard her whispering how divine he was to her sister. And each time, Jacqueline shared her amusement at him fulfilling his side of their bet. Even though they had never finished their game, he wanted to bring her joy.

Along the way, Falcone had noticed the attention he paid Lady Noel and shifted his attention to her. So at the last shop, she showed her displeasure when he offered to carry her box. It would appear he had fallen out of her favor. Kincaid only felt relief. Now he no longer had to endure her longing glances.

The ladies paused outside of a bookstore. Now this was one stop he wouldn't moan at following them into. His love of books matched

Jacqueline's and Lady Eden's. The previous stores they shopped in had stretched his patience with the ladies' inability to make a decision. Not to mention his annoyance with Lord Falcone. He held no opinion on what color ribbon they should purchase or which shade of thread used to embroider handkerchiefs with. Lord Falcone, however, was more than willing to offer his advice. The marquess's ability to charm each lady bothered Kincaid, especially when he directed his attention on Jacqueline. He knew Falcone did so to bait him into reacting, but he refused to ruin this excursion for Jacqueline.

Kincaid quickened his pace when Falcone opened the door for the ladies. The gentleman was always one step ahead of him at showcasing his manners. Jacqueline trailed behind the other ladies, glancing over her shoulder at Kincaid. A secretive smile graced her lips, and with a small nod, she indicated for him to follow. That very smile he wished for caused him to stumble and drop the packages. He never took his gaze off her, and she giggled into her glove at his mishap. He smiled at her like the besotted, smitten fool he was. Then Lady Eden tugged Jacqueline inside the store, and he lost sight of her.

Before he knelt to pick up the packages, he glanced at Falcone, who quirked his brow in question, then smirked his victory before sauntering inside with the ladies.

Kincaid bent over to gather the packages. "Arrogant bounder," he muttered.

"Why have you left the ladies alone with Falcone?" Gray snarled from behind him.

Kincaid sighed. He walked over to the carriage and passed the packages to the footmen, then continued toward the bookshop. Jacqueline had sent him a message with her smile, and he didn't want to miss his chance with her. “They are not alone with him. The shopkeeper and other villagers are inside, too.”

“They may as well be alone with how familiar he has acted toward them,” Gray argued.

Kincaid stopped in his tracks and turned toward his friend. “Have you followed us all day?”

“No. Only for the past hour. I do not care for the attention he pays Abigail.”

Kincaid shook his head. “For everyone’s sake, do not call him out.”

Gray scowled. “Why not? Falcone needs to understand he has overstepped himself. Abigail is not his to pursue.”

“Nor is she yours. You have stated your position regarding her and you hold no right to stop another gentleman from courting her.”

Gray gritted his teeth and stepped close to Kincaid. Yet, his friend never wavered his stance. He spoke quietly so no one passing by heard him. “Not only Falcone, but you have overstepped, too. First with my cousin, and now with Abigail. You may soon be Jacqueline’s husband, but you are the one who holds no right to question my actions.”

Kincaid stood still while Gray let out his frustration. He placed a hand on his shoulder to calm him. “Easy, Gray. I only meant to offer my advice. Falcone is here to play a game at our expense. Do not show your hand. He only finds amusement when we react. As for Abigail, I believe you upset her when you make your demands on how she should behave or who she can talk to.”

Gray stalked away, running a hand through his hair. He turned back to Kincaid and nodded his acceptance. “Shall we join them?”

Gray didn’t wait for Kincaid to answer and continued stalking toward the bookstore. Kincaid followed him inside and searched for

Jacqueline. He watched Gray move closer to Abigail, and he shook his head at how quickly Gray forgot his advice. At least, Falcone wasn't anywhere near Abigail or Jacqueline. He didn't even try to locate the marquess and instead snuck behind Jacqueline. She stood reading a book near the back of the shop.

He slipped his arm around her waist and bent his head to place a soft kiss against the back of her neck. She sighed at his touch. When she didn't protest his attentions, he swept her behind the bookcase into a small hallway where the shopkeeper kept his inventory. Kincaid visited the shop frequently whenever he stayed at Colebourne Manor. He knew the number of visitors would keep the shopkeeper near the front.

He pressed Jacqueline against the wall. Her impish smile beckoned him to devour her. However, he stole a kiss instead. His tongue stroked her lips to open for him. When she did, he captured her sighs. He pulled away and cupped her cheeks, brushing his thumb across her lips. "I need you."

Jacqueline melted at Kincaid's declaration. He uttered those three words with such intensity, she felt them at the bottom of her soul. Her body shook with need. However, they couldn't act on their desires. "Why the delay, Lord Kincaid? I thought you might have returned to the manor."

She needed to distract him, or otherwise, he would continue to kiss her senseless and they would shock the local villagers with a scandal. Jacqueline regretted asking him as soon as he pulled away from her.

"Your damn cousin cannot keep his opinion to himself about Abigail. I do not blame the lady for wanting to leave." When Jacqueline gasped, Kincaid closed his eyes at his mistake. "Forgive me, my love. I do not wish for her to leave, only that I understand her frustration toward Gray. He is exasperating in how he believes he has control over her actions. Even if they were married, it is not his right. But hers."

Once again, Jacqueline sighed at Kincaid. He truly was her knight in shining armor. The need to keep her independence was a powerful reason that she fooled herself into denying his marriage proposals. But all along, her heart knew he would never make demands of her. He might offer his suggestion, but he would leave the ultimate decision to her.

Kincaid cringed when Jacqueline remained silent. He'd blundered it when he spoke of Abigail so freely. He risked a glance in her direction and found her gazing at him with adoration. Somehow, he'd seemed to redeem himself when he mentioned Abigail's independence was her own and no other's. His declaration must have resonated with Jacqueline. Or at least, he hoped.

"Lord Kincaid?" Jacqueline whispered. She held up a finger and motioned for him to move closer.

"Mmm." His feet moved on their own accord.

She tugged on his cravat to draw him to her. Her hand slid around his neck, and she urged his head lower. He complied, and Jacqueline drew his lips between hers and kissed him, leaving him with no doubt.

Only hope.

Before he could wrap his arms around her, she slipped from his grasp and snuck back into the shop. Every few steps, she glanced behind her to see if he followed.

And he did, close on her heels. Before they encountered anyone, he whispered, "Minx." Her response was a throaty laugh, and she blew him a kiss.

A kiss he captured and allowed to soak into his senses. Her playfulness gave him a surge of hope. Even Falcone couldn't ruin his mood. When the lord approached Jacqueline and gave her suggestions, Kincaid trusted in his love. Because when he allowed Falcone to make him jealous, he showed Jacqueline that he didn't trust her, but he trusted her with his heart.

However, he wished he could say the same for his friend. After Kincaid didn't react to him, Falcone moved on to Abigail. Gray had taken a stand close to Abigail. He guarded her as if she were the queen herself. When Falcone reached for the book at the same moment as Abigail and their fingers touched, Gray advanced on them. He pulled Abigail away, standing between them.

"Lord Falcone, you take liberties not allowed with Miss Cason." Gray snarled.

Abigail gasped. "Lord Gray!"

"Stay out of this, Abigail," Gray ordered.

Abigail yanked her hand out of Gray's grasp and ran from the bookstore. Jacqueline and the Worthington sisters followed her. Kincaid stepped forward and tried to draw Gray back, but he wouldn't budge.

Kincaid attempted to smooth the matter over. "Gentlemen, shall we continue this later? You are drawing unwanted attention onto us, which will only cause rumors to spread about Miss Cason. Which I do not think either of you wishes upon the lady."

Falcone threw Gray a look. "On this, I will agree with you, Kincaid. I have no wish to tarnish the lady's reputation. It is a shame how others view her as it is. Especially when Gray subjects Miss Cason to his insensitive nature."

Gray growled, biting back his response. He wanted to pummel the arse in front of him, but he refused to have any gossip attached to Abigail's name. He'd already risked too much with his familiar grasp when he pulled her away. By all rights, his actions were no more different from Falcone's.

He turned and left the store. He needed to find Abigail and offer his apologies.

Which left Kincaid alone with Falcone. There was much he wanted to say to the marquess, but an audience had gathered to watch an altercation between two lords. He refused to give them a show or for Falcone to gloat his satisfaction at winning. Kincaid left the shop before Falcone could taunt a reaction from him.

When he came upon the carriage, Jacqueline was talking with Eden and Noel. Her worried expression caused him alarm. "Has something happened?"

"Abigail wanted to walk back to Colebourne Manor, and Lord Gray stormed off after her," Lady Eden explained.

Kincaid quirked a brow at Jacqueline. "Do you wish for me to follow them?"

Jacqueline shook her head. "No, 'tis best if my cousin digs himself a deeper hole. He will never learn otherwise. I think we should return. We are drawing attention our way."

Kincaid felt the stares focused on them. He helped the ladies into the carriage and joined them. He had seen Lord Falcone saunter off to the local tavern after he caused the scene in the bookstore. Tension hung over them during the ride back, a much different mood from when they left that morning. While he tried to make small talk, it all fell flat. Jacqueline kept a pensive expression, and he understood her grief. She felt torn between her cousin and her close friend, wanting them to settle their differences and admit their love for one another.

However, it would take the mischief of a matchmaking duke to perform that miracle.

~~~~~
~~~~~

Abigail stormed toward the manor. Lucas had followed her since she left the village. The humiliation of him attacking Lord Falcone over an innocent mistake flooded her with shame. How dare he! With each step she took, her fury grew. She wanted to turn and attack him with her wrath, but it was pointless. Lord Gray was an exasperating, arrogant, controlling arse. How she imagined herself in love with him confused even her.

Well, no more. She would harden her heart against him. She swiped at the tears pouring along her cheeks. Abigail hated how sensitive she was. She cried at the drop of the hat when something injured her emotions. During the past few months, Lord Gray had attacked her senses with each demand he made. Demands he made because he cared about her. Abigail understood why he said what he did, but it still caused her heart to ache. Except for now, his silence softened her heart.

Abigail knew Lucas kept his distance because he worried about her and understood how he'd hurt her. He would see her safely home, and she would forgive him as she always did. However, another piece of her heart had broken away today at his callous disregard. By now, Abigail doubted they even held a connection. It was all a figment of her imagination. Everyone told her to hold on to her faith in Lucas. But with each day that passed without his confession, her hope unraveled more.

Abigail stopped near the tall oak tree at the edge of the drive and waited for Lucas. When he reached her, she started walking again. Neither of them spoke. His guilt and her surrender at her circumstance hung between them. His behavior today showed Abigail how much she needed to take the governess position. She would proceed with her plans. It was the only way to keep her sanity.

When she waited for him, Gray realized she offered her forgiveness. He also realized his actions in the bookshop had helped Abigail make her decision to leave. He wanted to curse everyone and everything for his frustration. His father, his cousins, his friends, but most of all himself. He was the only one to blame for hurting her so deeply. The sight of the tears streaked along her cheeks settled in his gut. Guilt hovered overhead, ready to smother him.

He fought his need to draw her into his embrace. They were near the house and anyone would see. Not that she would allow him to comfort her. In the last few months, he had ruined their friendship. Each comment meant to protect her only slandered her instead. He was clueless about how to repair their friendship to the way it had been before his father started his matchmaking madness.

They reached the house, and Abigail paused on the steps. She turned and gazed at him with her sadness. He wanted to sink to his knees and plead his case. But she wouldn't give him a chance.

Abigail searched Lucas's eyes. She saw not only his guilt but also the longing that she herself felt. She offered him a small smile before walking through the door Oakes held open for them.

"Abigail?" Lucas asked softly.

Her only answer was to shake her head before she climbed the stairs and disappeared into the manor. Lucas's shoulders slumped in dejection.

He'd lost her.

Chapter Sixteen

Jacqueline stared out into the garden, watching Griffen saunter deeper into the lush oasis. That was how she viewed the garden, a paradise to lose oneself in. There were many twists, turns, and hidden spots to hide in. Trees and bushes filled every spot with their greenery. Flowers decorated the garden with amazing colors when in full bloom. She tracked the direction Griffen traveled by the lantern he carried. The soft light beckoned her to follow him.

When he waited for them in the foyer this morning, she'd realized he meant to fulfill his terms of the bet even though they'd never finished their game. He'd even kept his irritation in check when Lord Falcone joined them and never once gave Jacqueline any reason to ask him to leave. He'd kept his distance from the marquess, showing Jacqueline why she fell in love with him. Jacqueline smiled, remembering how he'd carried every package Lady Noel purchased. After each purchase, Jacqueline had giggled behind her gloved hand at his gallantry. However, Noel had muttered her frustration at his attention. It seemed the lady had moved her infatuation away from Griffen and to Lord Falcone. The marquess now held the title of the most divine. She wondered if Griffen suffered a bruised ego. She highly doubted so, but one never knew.

He'd never visited her bedchamber the previous evening, and she realized how complicated the madness of their relationship was. While he poured out his soul to her, she refused to do the same. By holding herself back, she filled his heart with doubt.

Did she have the nerve to fulfill her end of the bet? After all, she'd only promised him a midnight stroll through the gardens, nothing more. However, it was the scandalous bet that tempted Jacqueline to steal away into the night with Griffen. The whispered promise of wicked acts urged Jacqueline to follow him. She slipped on her robe and stole through the secret passageway and into the garden. She knew he waited in the secret spot they had deemed theirs. They had shared many intimate moments wrapped in a cocoon of the garden's wildness. And this evening, they would create more pleasurable memories.

Jacqueline took off on a run, eager for Griffen to hold her. She wanted him with an ache that overtook her senses. Every second without him caused an arrow to pierce her soul, tearing it wide apart. Only his touch would soothe her gaping wound. Only his kiss would comfort the pain. Only his whispered words of love would heal her broken soul.

Griffen heard the soft footsteps hurrying along the path, and his heartbeat quickened. When he left his room, he'd allowed hope to guide him toward their secret hiding spot. He'd refused to glance at her window to see if she watched him. He didn't intend to make her feel obligated to fulfill the bet when he'd honored his side of the wager. Griffen had done so because he knew Jacqueline would find amusement from the simple act. And every smile and giggle showed she had. Now he stood waiting with his vulnerable heart for any attention she might show him.

He stepped out of the shadows and onto the path. The white robe she wore shimmered in the moonlight, flowing behind her as she came closer toward him. Her beauty held him spellbound. It wasn't until she drew closer that he stepped forward and swept her into his arms, twirling her around as his lips met hers.

Their kiss started out slow and sensual, each of them falling into the bliss of their passion. His lips drew her sighs in while she absorbed his moans of pleasure. Slowly, their tongues stroked one another, drawing their need to new heights. Griffen lifted Jacqueline into his arms and stole into their sanctuary. He lowered her to the ground onto the blanket he had prepared earlier with the hope she would follow.

He pulled away from the kiss, brushing her hair back. His fingers trailed across her cheek as he stared at her in amazement. The soft light of the lantern cast a warm glow around her. Her arrival left him speechless, unable to describe his emotions. Every time she gave herself to him, she affected him profoundly. It was in these moments Jacqueline let her guard down, and he felt honored she trusted him enough to bare her soul.

Jacqueline trembled under Griffen's intense gaze. He'd regarded her in the same manner when they made love before. Yet, this evening, the mood had shifted. Her senses heightened to a new level she'd never experienced with him, causing her ache to grow unbearable. His gentle touch trailed over her cheek and up to tuck a strand of hair behind her ear.

He bent his head and pressed his lips under her ear, whispering, "You came."

His warm breath against her neck caused a shiver to race through her with anticipation of the scintillating pleasure to come. His stare raked her body, boldly undressing her. His eyes transformed in color, changing from a soft blue sea to a turbulent storm of desire. But he held himself back from the storm with steely determination.

While Jacqueline wished he would unleash his wildness and wreak his destruction on her soul, she realized she needed him to breathe his love into her and soothe the battle her soul fought to hold. She no longer wanted to keep hold of her love, but allow his love to consume her with its powerful need. Jacqueline wanted Griffen to hold the power in his hands.

Griffen knew the exact moment when Jacqueline surrendered to his love. It shone from her eyes when her emotions clicked into place. She softened under his touch and reached for him, drawing his head down to kiss her again.

Jacqueline brushed her lips across his before whispering into their kiss, "Yes. Now love me. My body yearns for your touch. For the taste of your lips on mine. For our souls to join as one. I need you, Griffen."

"You have bewitched me." Griffen's voice trembled with awe.

His soul-declaring whisper washed over Jacqueline. When he swept the nightgown off her, his touch set her on fire. She burned from his gentle caresses that drew out her ache to an unbearable torment.

She tore at his clothing, needing to feel his skin against hers. His hard body pressed into her softness, staking his claim. Jacqueline needed him to possess her heart and soul. She swept his shirt off and pressed her palms to his chest, his heat searing her. When she pressed her lips against his rapidly beating heart, the vibration sent a tingling sensation through her. Her fingers fumbled with the buttons on his breeches.

"Damn buttons," she muttered as they resisted her attention.

Griffen chuckled at the curse his temptress let out. "Allow me."

He guided her fingers, allowing each button to slide out of its hole before moving to the next one. When they finished with the buttons, their hands slid to his cock and released it into the open air. He hissed as her hand stroked under his. Her soft touch brought him to the brink of a desire he must satisfy if she continued. He tried to pull her hand to his mouth, but she would have none of it. She rose to her knees and pressed him back onto the blanket.

"Jacqueline," he moaned.

Before she lowered her head, a wickedly seductive smile graced her lips. Those lips soon hindered him incapable of denying either of them. She offered him no gentle teasing. Instead, her mouth devoured him with one swift slide down the length of his cock. Her tongue left a trail of fire the deeper she took him in. Over and over she tormented him with the exquisite strokes. Each demanded his surrender.

He looked down his body at the siren who sent him spiraling to the unknown. He didn't care as long as she never left his side. She captured his gaze as her tongue twirled near the tip, licking his wetness onto her tongue before sucking the tip of his cock in her mouth. Her lips molded around him, tempting him with anticipation of pleasure.

"My God," he moaned into the night, his body shaking with a need to release.

She lowered her lashes coyly before sliding him inside her mouth deeper, her hair billowing around her. Her long tresses brushed across his thighs with every plunge.

Jacqueline sensed Griffen losing control with each stroke of her tongue. Her mouth curved into a smile at his incomprehensible praises. Griffen was a very skilled lover who always seduced her with his wicked promises. To have him unable to speak a coherent word while she made love to him brought her much delight. The proper viscount who always showed his ability to appear most dignified unraveled before her.

His hands sank into her hair, guiding her to his pleasure. At each pull of her lips, she struck a chord in him. Pleasing him intensified a need in her that only Griffen could appease.

With one last kiss, she slid up his body and whispered, "Love me, Griffen."

He rolled them over and ravished her mouth. His cock pressed into her core, and she bucked her hips against him, wanting him inside her. However, he would deny her and strike out with his own blissful torment.

Griffen wanted to take his time and draw out their desires in slow, agonizing caresses until Jacqueline writhed underneath him, begging for him to take her. While her body already made those demands, he hungered to savor her sweetness in return. His need overtook him and staked his claim with every kiss and caress he brushed across her velvety skin.

Griffen held her breasts in her hands while his tongue teased them, pulling them between his lips and nipping at them. Moving back and forth between the luscious buds, he savored their sweetness. Their flavor only enticed him to slowly move his kisses lower.

"Griffen," Jacqueline moaned. "Please."

"Please what, love?"

"Love me." Her fingers feathered through his hair.

"But I am."

"No, you are tormenting me with your kisses."

He kissed her. "Patience, my love."

Before Jacqueline could voice her objections again, Griffen slid his hand between her thighs and to her wetness. She coated him with her need. He brushed his thumb across her clit and heard her breath hitch. When he slid a finger inside her, Jacqueline whimpered a moan. He lowered himself between her legs, his head dipping to her core, and stroked his tongue along her center.

Her thighs clamped around his head, and her fingers dove into his hair, holding him to her. Griffen's appetite grew ravenous at the first lick and wouldn't find satisfaction until he devoured her. His tongue struck out, drawing forth her release.

Jacqueline floated away at the sensations Griffen drew from her body. With each slide of his finger and lick of his wicked tongue, her body fed him with her desires. Still, it wasn't enough for him. He wanted more. She didn't think she could meet his needs. However, her body surprised her by gifting him with her trust. With his tongue flickering back and forth, he slid another finger inside her and played her like a violin. Jacqueline cried out as he sent her flying.

Griffen rose above her with a wickedly smug expression. Then he slid inside her and she forgot every coherent thought in her head. Griffen surrounded her, wrapping her within his soul. He drove them to new heights, and Jacqueline clung to him, hoping he would never let her go.

He stared into Jacqueline's eyes, never once losing sight of the expressions crossing her delicate features as he loved her. She was the most beautiful thing he'd ever seen. Love filled her gaze, and it warmed his soul. He didn't need her to whisper the words when her body expressed them. When she was ready, she would tell him. All he could offer her was his patience. In the meantime, he needed to express his love for her.

"I love you," he whispered.

Tears streamed from Jacqueline's eyes at his tender words. He linked their hands together while he sent them soaring into an unchartered atmosphere. He lowered his head, kissing each tear away, and gathered Jacqueline close.

"Griffen?" Jacqueline trembled his name.

"Shh. Let me hold you before we must return. There will be time later."

"Will there?"

"Yes."

Jacqueline's fingers tightened around his. "Do you promise?"

"I promise."

He heard the fear in her voice, but he had no words to calm her. A promise was all he could make until she trusted in their love. He would patiently wait for her to do so.

They lay in each other's arms, staring up at the stars. Griffen whispered soft endearments, reassuring her of his affection. When the moon dipped to welcome the sun, he helped her dress and wrapped her in a blanket. Then he carried her back to the manor. By the time he laid Jacqueline on her bed, she had fallen asleep. He pulled the covers over her and sat watching her sleep. He brushed the hair from her forehead and leaned down to place a kiss.

"Sweet dreams, my love. I hope you fill them with me."

Chapter Seventeen

Gray rudely woke Kincaid the next morning by throwing open the drapes and shoving him in the shoulder. "Wake up, Kincaid."

He threw the covers over his head. "Sod off."

Gray laughed at Kincaid's surliness. "I cannot. I am here to drag your arse out of bed."

"What in the hell for?"

"Fishing."

Kincaid moaned. His late evening with Jacqueline had exhausted him. After he carried her inside, he'd stayed by her bed, watching her sleep. His insecurities had grown the longer he stayed. He feared she would reject his offer, and he held an odd feeling that she planned to end their relationship after the hunt. He didn't know how to convince her to give them a chance other than professing his love in front of her entire family. It wouldn't end well for him if he did. He didn't want to go fishing. First, he wanted to finish sleeping. Then he wanted to find Jacqueline and propose, hoping she changed her answer to yes.

He opened an eye. "I will pass."

"No, you will not. Get up, this is your only chance to gain my father's blessing for Jacqueline's hand."

Kincaid sat up, reaching for his trousers. He pulled them on, shooting out of bed and finished dressing before Gray continued with his explanation. He yanked on his boots, gathered his old coat, and strode out the door. Kincaid glanced over his shoulder to see Gray staring at him with a frown. "Are you coming?"

Gray shook his head at Kincaid's eagerness. He hoped to explain his plan to Kincaid, but his friend didn't allow him one word of explanation. He could only follow when Kincaid flew down the stairs. Gray wanted to warn Kincaid that his father hadn't invited him, but he would find out for himself. It served him right for seducing his cousin.

They walked toward the stables and came to a stop when his father called out to them from atop his chosen mount. "When you mentioned fishing, you never said you would bring the bait."

Ramsay cackled. "I have never used bait like this before."

"Oh, we should get quite a few bites with him," Colebourne replied.

Kincaid narrowed his gaze at Gray. "Blessing, huh?"

Gray shrugged. "It is worth a try."

"Even if I was not invited," Kincaid muttered.

"Nay, you were not. But grab a pole. Daylight is wasting away," Colebourne ordered and galloped away with Ramsay.

Gray and Kincaid grabbed the poles and followed on their horses. He heard the older gentlemen quarreling about which pond to fish at. Gray had tricked him into joining them.

"Why?"

Gray sighed. "Because you need my father's attention without the distractions of the houseguests. He is most relaxed when he is fishing."

"I thought you were against my union with Jacqueline."

Gray's hands tightened around the reins before relaxing. "You overstepped our bounds of friendship, but then I realized you did not differ from Worthington. I would rather my cousins settle with my friends than with gentlemen who I am unsure of their character. Also, I do not care how my father interferes with his matchmaking by using Falcone as a pawn in his madness. If I can help you and Jacqueline settle, then I can refocus on Abigail. The longer Falcone remains in residence, the more of a threat he remains."

Kincaid nodded. "I understand, but you could have least warned me."

Gray scoffed. "You never gave me a chance. You scurried out of your bedchamber in such a rush."

Kincaid laughed. "That I did." He grew serious, reaching out his hand. "Thank you."

Gray shook Kincaid's hand. The guilt at setting his friend up for his father's refusal only caused him to cringe for a minute. Then it quickly disappeared because all was fair in love and war. And he fought to keep Abigail from a life of servitude. While he couldn't offer her marriage, he refused to allow her to become a servant. If he kept his father distracted with Jacqueline and Kincaid, then he could persuade Abigail to turn down the offer she'd received to become a governess. He would have to enlist the help of Gemma, but he had the perfect solution to keep Abigail nearby.

Kincaid and Gray guided their horses toward the tree and joined Colebourne and Ramsay for a morning of fishing. Everyone stayed silent, which was a rare occurrence for the older gentlemen. Kincaid soon grew drowsy from the lack of entertainment. A few times, he drifted to sleep under the warm sun, but Gray would nudge him back awake. The last time it happened, his gaze connected with Colebourne, who shook his head in disappointment. When Colebourne moved to another spot across the pond, Kincaid debated on following him. But when the duke scowled in his direction, he remained in his spot.

"Do you want the lass or not?" Ramsay asked.

Kincaid sighed. "Yes."

Ramsay nodded. "Then you best get yourself over there and start groveling."

"It was the reason I brought him with us," Gray muttered.

"They have the bollocks to seduce the lasses but cower when up against an old coot."

Kincaid bristled. "I am not afraid of Colebourne."

Ramsay shrugged. "What are ye waiting for, an invitation? This isn't a debutante ball, it is your future, boy."

Kincaid drew his pole out of the water, shooting Ramsay a glare at his taunts. He trudged around the pond to sit next to Colebourne. The duke didn't show any expression at his arrival and continued to fish, not catching a single thing. Kincaid threw his pole in and, within a few minutes, caught a fish. Colebourne harrumphed but stayed silent.

When Kincaid caught another fish, Colebourne blurted out his objections. "Not only did you steal my remaining unwed niece, but must you steal all the fish, too?"

Kincaid looked at him with exasperation. "You invited me here in the spring for the sole purpose of becoming Jacqueline's husband."

Colebourne pinched his lips. "Well, I might have changed my mind."

Kincaid panicked. If he couldn't get Colebourne's support, it would only make Jacqueline more hesitant to accept his proposal. The future he planned for them was disappearing before his very eyes.

Colebourne took pity on Kincaid. "Calm down."

Kincaid stormed away, only to return seconds later. "How do you expect me to calm down when you plan to reject my suit of Jacqueline? I love her, and I cannot imagine my life without her. Ever since we shared our first kiss, I knew she was the lady I wanted to marry. To win her hand and your approval, I knew I must climb out of debt. I developed a brilliant business idea and then you pulled your support away for no plausible reason."

Colebourne growled. "I had plenty of reasons."

"Name one."

Colebourne leaned back against the rock and crossed his arms. "You said so yourself, the first kiss you shared with Jacqueline. Why are you kissing my niece when you are not married?"

Kincaid sputtered. "It was… She asked… I…"

"Exactly. Not to mention, I know more than kissing transpires between you and Jacqueline."

Kincaid threw his hands in the air. "All the more reasons to give your blessing."

Colebourne bit out a sarcastic laugh. "Is that your only defense? Then my standing remains the same."

Kincaid realized his mistake the minute he spoke, but he was powerless to stop them. He'd never wanted to win Jacqueline's hand by telling the duke of their affair. While Colebourne only baited him, it was a test on how Kincaid would react. And he'd reacted miserably. The seriousness on Colebourne's face displayed the severity of their discussion. His chance at redeeming himself had blown away with the wind.

He swiped a hand down his face. "My apologies. I am at my wit's end, and I have no clue how to act. My greatest wish is for your blessing in asking Jacqueline to become my wife. I understand I scandalously ruined her. But I do not regret one moment with her. Nor will I allow her to suffer any shame. The love we share is rare."

Colebourne pointed at the rock next to him. “Take a seat,” he ordered.

Kincaid sat against the rock, waiting for Colebourne to speak. However, the duke only picked up his pole and started fishing again without a word. After a while, Kincaid followed his lead and fished again. Time passed, and the sun climbed higher in the sky.

Kincaid looked across the pond and caught Gray’s questioning stare, and he shrugged. He watched Gray and Ramsay shake with laughter at the conversation they held. Snippets floated across the pond. Kincaid caught the words of “a scoundrel,” “ruined an innocent,” “rake of the highest order.” He glared across at them, and their teasing grew louder. Kincaid felt uncomfortable the longer the silence hovered between Colebourne and him. He dared a glance and saw the duke hiding a grin at the humor. Kincaid blew out a pent-up breath he hadn’t even realized he’d held.

“And he calls himself a friend,” Kincaid muttered.

“Only one’s friend can find humor in another friend’s mistakes.”

Kincaid turned his head. “You have a point.”

Colebourne smiled smugly. “I always do.”

“How can I change your mind?”

Colebourne shook his head. “There is no need, my son. It is I who owes you an explanation.”

Kincaid’s eyebrows drew together in confusion. “How so?”

“I invited you amongst the other chosen gentlemen to a house party in the spring to make matches with my nieces. And one by one, I made those matches. Each lady fell in love and got married. Before I knew it, my household grew smaller and, I must confess, lonelier.”

Kincaid scoffed. “How could you possibly be lonely with so much drama always surrounding you?”

Colebourne laughed. "True, and it is most welcome. Still, sadness set in when I faced losing Jacqueline. She has always been the rock of our family, especially when I have needed her. I suppose, in my selfishness, I reacted badly when I watched her fall in love with you and knew she would leave for a new home. One she deserves and needs. So, I am asking for your forgiveness."

"I forgive you. However, why did you withdraw your support from my business venture? You showed interest in its success."

"I am. But I knew I couldn't offer you the same resources as Ralston could. Plus, it was a perfect match for his and Worth's detective service."

Kincaid nodded. "You dropped hints for Gray to mention it to Ralston."

Colebourne harrumphed. "That boy can take a hint for everything except for what truly matters."

Kincaid looked over at his friend. "Oh, I believe he is aware of the hints thrown at him, but his stubbornness resists them."

"I believe you are correct. But that is another matter to tackle after I get you and Jacqueline settled."

Hope flared in Kincaid's eyes. "You will offer your support."

"Aye."

"Thank you. I am indebted to you with gratitude."

Colebourne sighed. "No. There is no debt with family. Your days of fulfilling your obligations because of your mishaps as a youth are now clear. I have another confession to make. I promised your father before he died that I would look out for you. And over the years, I did. That was before a gaggle of young ladies overcame my days. Then I neglected to keep up with your activities. When I bailed you out from the trouble with the Duke of

Gostwicke, it was to keep you within sight. However, it kept you from rising to your full potential. But over the past three years, I've noticed a new spark within you. Is Jacqueline the reason?"

"Yes. She makes me strive to be a better man."

"A diamond of a lady will hold that effect over a man. Jacqueline reminds me of my Olivia. Maybe that is why I struggle to let her go," Colebourne whispered.

"You are not losing her. You only have to share her. You will always be a part of our lives, and I promise we shall visit often. So frequently you will tire of us." Kincaid paused and then admitted, "Since we are confessing our secrets, I must confess how much I appreciated your guidance over the years, and I hope it continues."

"Take my advice and tell Jacqueline the truth about your past before it is too late."

"Is that why you invited Falcone?"

Colebourne stared at Kincaid with no regret for his actions. "Yes, and he has his own obligation to fulfill. So, I would not hesitate any longer."

"How many of us do you have under your thumb?"

Colebourne laughed. "More than you would believe."

"What if I am too late?"

"You could very possibly be. I gave him a deadline, and it is fast approaching. Why, even now, Falcone could reveal your secret."

Kincaid jumped to his feet. "Then why are we still fishing?"

Not waiting for an answer, he grabbed both of their poles and the fish he'd caught. He held out his other hand for Colebourne and helped him to rise. Then, with quick strides, he walked around the pond and ordered the other gentlemen to hurry. "We must leave now."

Colebourne followed Kincaid slowly, amused at his need to rush back to the manor. "Calm down, boy. Falcone is probably still abed and hasn't spoken to Jacqueline yet."

Kincaid spun around. "You have no clue what that blinder is capable of. He will gladly ruin my relationship with Jacqueline and take pleasure from the outcome. He is ruthless and will show no mercy with her feelings."

Colebourne pondered Kincaid's words and knew he stood correct. He hadn't taken into count how unscrupulous the gentleman was when he invited Falcone. Perhaps his son was right, and he had taken this whole matchmaking business too far. To date, he'd been lucky with the outcomes, but Jacqueline was harder to coerce. Her fear and stubbornness kept her from finding happiness. Now, when she might have taken a chance on Kincaid, Colebourne had ruined it with his games.

He hurried to the horses, throwing over his shoulder, "You heard the boy. We must return to the manor immediately."

Ramsay and Gray shook their heads at one another but followed behind them. During the ride back, Gray convinced them they were overreacting about Falcone. Ramsay even threw in his odd attempt at humor, calming Kincaid and Colebourne. Soon, the group was laughing and bantering back and forth. Once they reached the stables, they handed their horses and fishing gear off to the stable boys. They trudged up to the house and entered through the garden entrance, where they met Lady Forrester talking to the butler.

"Here ye go, Oakes. Take these to Cook for luncheon." Ramsay handed off the fish.

Oakes turned up his nose at the disturbing odor. "Very well, my lord."

Lady Forrester laughed. “That is quite a catch.”

Ramsay nodded toward Kincaid. “He can catch the fish, just not the lady.”

Gray laughed at his uncle’s slander. “Give the bloke a break, he is using the wrong bait with Jacqueline.”

Colebourne tilted his head toward the garden, where Jacqueline hurried along the path. “Here is his chance.”

Chapter Eighteen

Jacqueline sat on a bench in the garden with a smile. Her gaze kept straying to where Griffen had made passionate love to her. She had cried at the end, and he'd comforted her without needing to understand why her tears fell. His unspoken acceptance made her realize the depth of his love. The emotions their lovemaking invoked had overwhelmed her. Even when Griffen declared his love, he'd done so because he needed to voice his emotion, not to hear the sentiment in return.

She'd awoken this morning eager to declare her love. After eating breakfast in Evelyn's bedchamber, she'd rushed belowstairs to find Griffen. But to her disappointment, she couldn't find him anywhere. When she came upon Aunt Susanna, she told her Griffen had joined Ramsay, Lucas, and Uncle Theo for fishing. She didn't know when they would return. Jacqueline's heart warmed at this news. It meant Uncle Theo once again thought Griffen was suitable.

Now she waited near their secret hideaway, hoping he would seek her out upon his return. However, she wasn't alone. Lord Falcone had requested for Abigail and her to walk with him in the garden again. They'd agreed. Only this time, she'd convinced Eden to join them, too. Falcone and Abigail separated from them to discuss the flowers, as they had on their previous walk. It didn't bother Jacqueline in the slightest because then she could lose herself in her memories of Griffen.

He made her heart race like no other. His kisses warmed her insides, and his caresses built her desires higher. But it was his loving embrace Jacqueline found the most comfort in. It wrapped her securely in his arms, showing her the protection he offered from her greatest fears in the best way he knew how. It was in his embrace that her fears disappeared. She rested her hand on her stomach, eager to share her news with him. And her love.

"I hope Abigail is not falling for Lord Falcone's false charms?" Eden muttered.

Eden's question startled Jacqueline from her musings. She felt dreadful for ignoring her friend while she daydreamed about Griffen. She refocused her gaze on Abigail and Falcone. Abigail laughed at something the marquess said. While she appeared to enjoy herself, her smile never reached her eyes. No. Abigail wasn't falling for Falcone. Lucas's stubbornness still tore her apart.

"No, I think the gentleman is only a welcome distraction."

"That is a relief. I feared she'd fallen for his nefarious charms."

Jacqueline frowned. "Do you believe Lord Falcone is false with his regards?"

Eden scoffed. "The gentleman's every action is false."

"That is a harsh accusation. What reason do you have for your opinion? He has only ever acted like a gentleman toward me and Abigail."

Eden glared at Falcone. "All an act, my dear friend. I don't understand what his true motive is, but believe me, he has one."

Jacqueline tried to laugh at Eden's declaration, but her friend truly believed the worst about Falcone. "You are serious?"

Eden turned her gaze on Jacqueline. "Yes. I have watched my brothers use the same finesse on countless ladies, so I know a rake when I see one."

Jacqueline nodded in understanding, even though she didn't hold the same opinion of Falcone's deception. Eden acted out of friendly concern for Abigail's welfare, and that alone was touching. Abigail needed all the friendly acceptance she could gather.

She patted Eden's hand. "You are a kind friend. Do not worry, though. Abigail has already lost her heart to my cousin and will not allow herself to feel any affection for another gentleman. No matter how kind or charming they may be."

"Your cousin is a fool."

Jacqueline chuckled. "I agree."

Jacqueline's amusement drew Abigail and Lord Falcone over to them. They stood in front of Jacqueline and Eden with curiosity written across their faces. Eden's look of displeasure toward Falcone, who was oblivious to it, only made Jacqueline chuckle harder.

"May we inquire about your amusement?" Lord Falcone asked.

"Oh, we were discussing the merits of what made a gentleman a rake. Present company included," Eden taunted.

Falcone quirked a brow. "Please tell. I am most interested in the details of my questionable character."

Eden bristled. "Sorry, but it is a private discussion between ladies."

Falcone clutched at his heart dramatically, earning a giggle from Abigail. "You will not even allow me to defend myself?"

"What, with more false declarations of your charm? I know your style, Lord Falcone. You ply ladies with promises and seduce them with your wicked words, only to break their hearts when you tire of them."

A wicked smile drifted over Falcone's lips. "I did not realize you thought so highly of me."

Eden hissed. "Do not flatter yourself."

"Oh, but I do."

Falcone rocked on his heels with a smirk as Eden kept opening and closing her hands into fists. Jacqueline shivered at the animosity rolling off Eden and smacking Falcone in amusement. The air sizzled around them. She needed to repair their visit and play peacemaker, a skill she had perfected over the years with her family and their disagreements.

"Are you enjoying your stay at Colebourne Manor?"

"Yes, I am." Falcone never once turned his stare away from Eden.

Abigail tried to help Jacqueline with the awkward situation. "Lord Falcone shared with me his excitement for the hunt."

"I offer my apologies if my company has offended you, ladies. But in my defense, I don't see how I differ from the other gentlemen in residence. Especially considering Lord Kincaid's reputation."

Eden jumped to his defense. "Lord Kincaid's reputation is impeccable. He is an honorable gentleman."

Falcone pinched his lips. "Which only proves my point of how innocent you ladies are. You cannot see the difference between a gentleman whose only purpose is to seduce you into a scandal from a gentleman who only entertains with harmless flirtation."

"Why, that is preposterous!" Eden harrumphed.

Jacqueline tilted her head in confusion. "Are you implying Lord Kincaid has ulterior motives?"

"Yes. It is my impression he does. He is a penniless viscount who seeks your uncle's purse for a business venture that is sure to fail. I only warn you because you are not the first lady he has fooled with his attention."

"Perhaps you are mistaken," Abigail said.

"I wish that were the case, as does my sister."

Jacqueline whispered, "Your sister?"

"Yes. Kincaid caused a rift in my sister's marriage with his irrefutable behavior. Then he made matters worse when he made a bet with her husband for her affections. One game of billiards almost destroyed her marriage all because he found boredom in the structure of our society. She amused him with her sweet and innocent nature. Your uncle might have stopped his foolishness, and he changed his image to a stand-up gentleman, but his true character will never change." He turned his attention back to Eden. "And that, Lady Eden, is an example of a rake with nefarious intentions."

"No, you are wrong," Jacqueline whispered in denial. Nothing Falcone spoke held any truth. The gentleman he described was one with a callous character, not the gentleman she'd fallen in love with.

"I am not." His voice echoed firmly.

Jacqueline searched his features for any sign that he spoke out of revenge, but his stare reflected what he thought to be facts, along with a hint of pity. Jacqueline kept shaking her head in denial. Her stomach recoiled at the disturbing information. She covered her mouth and bolted toward the manor.

"Excuse me." Abigail watched Jacqueline pale and hurried after Jacqueline, wanting to offer comfort.

"How could you?" Eden demanded.

"I thought it was in the best interest for Lady Jacqueline to learn of Lord Kincaid's character before he seduced her with his whispered promises. I do hope I am not too late," Falcone answered smugly.

Eden wanted to rant at his arrogance, but her mother had raised her to always act like a lady, even when someone might provoke her otherwise. Also, she refused to show Lord Falcone how much he infuriated her. Instead, she would question the validity of his accusation.

"You hold a strong vindictiveness toward Lord Kincaid for an action in the past not involving you."

"It involved my sister," he snarled.

Eden nodded. "Yes, it did. And does your sister still hold animosity for Lord Kincaid?"

Falcone paused, hesitating with his answer. He couldn't rightly say. He'd never asked his sister about the consequences of her involvement with Kincaid. It didn't matter anyhow. Kincaid was in the wrong. "It does not matter in the scope of his past behavior."

Eden rose and smoothed out her skirts. "Doesn't it, though? You cannot outright judge their interest in one another when you do not know the reasons behind their involvement. Only your sister and Lord Kincaid hold knowledge of the depth of what happened all those years ago. Your only knowledge is hearsay. Perhaps your sister gravitated towards Kincaid because she felt neglected and he offered her affection she found missing from her marriage. My point is, you had no right slandering Kincaid without him here to defend himself." With that said, Eden sauntered away, leaving Falcone to ponder over his affront.

Falcone watched the blonde vixen, enjoying the swish of her hips as she walked away. Lady Eden was a most tempting distraction, but one he must not indulge in if he favored his life. And he did. Her brother already doubted his undercover abilities. He didn't want to anger Graham Worthington by trifling with his sister. Also, innocents weren't quite his flavor. No, he liked women who purred at his every word. And all Lady Eden did was hiss.

However, her parting words struck his interest. The next time he paid his sister a visit, he must inquire the full details of her relationship with

Kincaid. While her marriage appeared happy and her husband doted on her, maybe it hadn't always been in that regard.

Either way, he'd accomplished what the duke ordered of him. While it might cause the other guests to treat him differently, it was for the best. After the hunt, he would travel back to the continent and finish his assignment while clearing another one of his debts to Colebourne.

Hopefully, his debts will be cleared soon.

~~~~~

Kincaid swung toward the open door to see Jacqueline's pale face streaming with tears. He started toward her, but once she saw him, she gasped and came to a stop. "Jacqueline, what has troubled you?"

Her eyes widened, and she covered her mouth again. Without answering, she flew past him and rushed up the stairs.

"Oh, my. I must see to Jacqueline's welfare." Lady Forrester followed her.

Colebourne set a hand on Kincaid's shoulder. "Get cleaned up, and I will arrange for you to talk with Jacqueline. In the meantime, I will discover what has upset her so."

Kincaid nodded, but he held little faith in Colebourne convincing Jacqueline to meet with him. Her hurt-filled gaze could only mean she'd already learned the truth from Falcone. She felt betrayed he hadn't confided in her.

Gray offered his own support after his father and Ramsay left. "Believe in your love, it will get you through this troubling mishap."

Kincaid became even more doubtful when Abigail rushed up the path and came to a halt before them. "Jacqueline?"

"What happened? She was white as a ghost," Kincaid asked.
~~~~~

She winced. "Lord Falcone told her some disturbing news."

"Sorry, mate."

Kincaid pinched his lips. "I only have myself to blame."

"Jacqueline tried to defend you, but Falcone remained adamant on what he perceived to be the truth," Lady Eden explained, walking up behind Abigail.

Kincaid raked a hand through his hair. "Which is the truth. If you will excuse me, I must try to speak with Jacqueline."

Abigail placed her hand on his sleeve. "You must give her time to herself. She is most upset, and I am afraid she will say something she might regret later. I must go to her."

Kincaid nodded, too choked to speak. His embarrassment caused him to walk away without another word. Now everyone had learned of his past misdeeds. He went to his bedchamber to change and found the servants filling the tub with warm water. Lady Forrester, while seeing to Jacqueline, also offered him some comfort, too. He would take Colebourne's advice and prepare to meet with Jacqueline. Hopefully, the duke could convince her to speak with him.

If not, he would wait patiently until she would.

Chapter Nineteen

Humiliation ricocheted through Jacqueline as she rushed upstairs. She reached her bedchamber just in time to empty her stomach. Not long after, a wet towel settled against her cheeks and comforting arms guided her toward the bed. She trembled from her sickness and the upsetting emotions Lord Falcone had invoked in her. Aunt Susanna whispered soft words of comfort and dried her tears. Jacqueline curled up in a ball and shivered uncontrollably. She heard Abigail arrive and question about her welfare, but their conversation sounded far away. She closed her eyes, trying to block out the past hour.

When she ran from the garden and encountered Griffen, she'd seen him laughing with her uncle, and his newfound hope swept off him in waves. She wanted to seek comfort in his arms, but her doubts froze her in place. As he drew closer, the odor from the fish filled the hallway and sent her stomach roiling. Falcone's accusation already sickened her, but the actual smell of the fish was more than her stomach could bear.

She heard Aunt Susanna leave, and Abigail settled in a chair by her bed. Jacqueline had no explanation to offer, nor did she want to discuss what she had learned. Abigail's silence soothed her frazzled emotions. She only hoped her sisters and Gemma wouldn't learn about her ordeal. Jacqueline wasn't ready to confess her secret to them.

She should have known better.

Evelyn and Gemma rushed in mere minutes later, asking over her welfare at once. Jacqueline swiped at her eyes. “I do not wish to discuss why I am upset.”

They looked toward Abigail for her to explain. “It is not my place, and I must abide by Jacqueline’s wishes.”

Evelyn nodded. “Then how can we help you?”

“I wish to stay overnight with Charlie. Can you help me prepare?”

“Of course we will,” Gemma answered.

Evelyn pulled Jacqueline’s valise from the wardrobe and packed her a few essentials for her stay while Abigail went to find a footman to ready a carriage. Once Evelyn finished, they walked down to the carriage. Jacqueline settled in the seat and turned to thank them, but Evelyn, Gemma, and Abigail climbed in to join her for the ride.

“There is no need for you to ride along.”

“Yes, there is. Something has upset you, and we wish to show our support as you have done over the years,” Evelyn explained.

Jacqueline swallowed, too choked to reply.

Abigail squeezed her hand. “It will all be well.”

Jacqueline bit her lip to keep from crying and stared out the window. The horses started off, and the comforting silence only a family could offer filled the carriage. At that point, Jacqueline didn’t know if Abigail’s words would ring true. How could they? She had fallen in love with a gentleman she didn’t even know. But didn’t she? She felt she understood Griffen better than she understood herself. Also, Falcone spoke of an incident from Griffen’s past, when she wasn’t a part of his life. However, the depravity of the situation bothered her. Was he capable of still behaving in the same manner?

When they arrived, the butler greeted them and showed them into the parlor. Charlie rushed into the room before they had even taken off their bonnets. "What do we owe this surprise? Jasper and I were preparing to ride over early for dinner."

"I do not mean to impose, but may I stay overnight?"

Charlie's eyebrows drew together, and she swept the room, but no one offered an explanation. She noticed the sadness in Jacqueline's gaze. "Of course. I will have a room prepared."

Before Jacqueline could tell her there was no rush, Charlie left the parlor. When she didn't return, Jacqueline wondered what kept her. In the meantime, a servant arrived and served them tea. The other ladies talked amongst themselves while Jacqueline kept replaying Falcone's accusation.

Minutes later, Charlie returned with Sinclair by her side. The lord wore a pensive look. Usually, when something troubled one of them, they kept it within their small circle of ladies. However, Charlie included her husband today, and Jacqueline was thankful for his calm demeanor. She and Sinclair shared a close friendship. Perhaps he could shed some light on her predicament.

Sinclair offered a comforting smile. "I hear you will be our guest for the evening. It will upset my mother to learn that she missed you. However, Charlie and I will enjoy your company."

Jacqueline attempted to return his smile but failed. "Thank you, Sinclair, for your kindness."

Charlie tilted her head to the side, allowing her shrewd gaze to settle on Jacqueline. Her sister was the most observant of them all and realized something was amiss. "What has he done? Tell me and I will have Jasper remove him from Uncle Theo's estate."

Sinclair laughed, guiding Charlie to sit down. He stood behind her. "We will not take decisive action against Kincaid when we don't know of his misstep."

A sob escaped Jacqueline.

"Do we?" Sinclair growled.

Jacqueline tried to explain, but her shoulders racked with sobs and tears streamed along her cheeks. Evelyn wrapped her arm around Jacqueline and drew her close. Evelyn nodded at Abigail to explain. Abigail sent Jacqueline a questioning stare, and Jacqueline nodded her acceptance.

"This afternoon during our walk in the garden with Lord Falcone, we fell into the discussion about disreputable gentlemen. Lady Eden baited the lord with indications that she referred to him. He took offense when she wouldn't allow him to defend himself."

Charlie laughed. "I take it Lady Eden does not find Lord Falcone to be an upstanding gentleman. I noticed the hostility she held toward him, but I attributed it to him not paying her any attention."

"My sister-in-law holds no interest in Lord Falcone, only displeasure at his pursuit of Abigail and the attention he pays Jacqueline when it is a known fact Uncle Theo has promised each lady to another gentleman," Evelyn explained.

Abigail bristled. "I am promised to no other gentleman. And I enjoy Lord Falcone's company immensely, and you can inform Eden so."

Evelyn cringed. "I did not mean to imply otherwise Abigail. I only state how Eden perceives your situation. On my return, I shall set her straight."

Abigail nodded. "Thank you. Please see that you do."

Sinclair cleared his throat. "This does not explain the reason for Jacqueline's turmoil and how it involves Kincaid."

"In his defense, Lord Falcone explained a scandal his sister became embroiled in because of Lord Kincaid's interest. His married sister, I might add," Abigail explained.

"Is Uncle Theo aware of Lord Kincaid's misdeeds?" Charlie asked.

Gemma scoffed. "I am sure our uncle is well aware of Kincaid's faults. He probably bailed him out of the situation, making him indebted to him as Ralston was."

"If that is the case, then Jasper will send him on his way." Charlie's voice rose with agitation.

Sinclair rested his hand on Charlie's shoulder. "Calm down, my love." He looked at Jacqueline. "Do you wish for Kincaid to leave?"

Jacqueline shrugged. "I am so confused. I do not see him capable of Lord Falcone's accusation. Maybe I don't know his true character as well as I thought I did."

Sinclair arched a brow. "Do you not?

Jacqueline stood up and paced around the parlor. "I am not so sure. How could he have acted as he did?"

"What did he do? Perhaps Lord Falcone is mistaken," Gemma asked.

Jacqueline stopped, facing them. "No, he was most adamant about Griffen's nefarious deeds. Even gloated when he slandered his name."

Jacqueline's temper rose the more she thought about Falcone's slander. Did Lord Falcone set out to destroy their relationship? And if so, why?

"The marquess spoke of how Griffen played a game of billiards with his sister's husband, making a bet for the sister's affection as the prize. If Griffen won, then he could continue to pursue an affair with the lady," Jacqueline explained.

Gemma and Evelyn gasped at the scandalous bet. Blushes spread across every lady's cheeks. Every lady but Charlie. Her scandalous behavior in the past prevented anything from shocking her.

"Oh, my. I clearly underestimated the viscount. And to think I thought he was a proper bore. My, my! He will keep your marriage interesting, dear sister." Charlie waggled her brows.

"Charlotte!" Evelyn exclaimed.

Charlie shrugged. "What? I only speak the truth. The viscount is a walking contradiction. Lady Noel had him right, he is most divine."

"No, he is most scandalous. And we were correct in making Jacqueline end their affair," Evelyn argued.

"Neither of you may make that decision. Only Jacqueline," Sinclair stated.

Abigail nodded. "I agree."

"As do I," Gemma seconded.

"What do you advise, Sinclair?" Jacqueline trusted his opinion. He wasn't only a friend but a brother due to his marriage to Charlie.

"I believe you should give him a chance to defend himself. It is obviously an occurrence in his past and doesn't reflect the gentleman he is today. If you don't believe him after he explains, then you will have your answer."

Jacqueline nodded. "I thought along the same lines, but I fear I allow my scattered emotions to make my judgements. I want to give him the benefit of the doubt, but I also fear the unknown."

Sinclair trailed his hand down Charlie's arm to clasp her hand. "That is understandable. Now, I am not defending Kincaid by any means. But as a gentleman who made many foolish mistakes in my youth, I ask that you do not judge him so harshly. After all, he is but a mere mortal and allowed imperfections."

Jacqueline's gaze followed Sinclair's hand and she smiled at the affection he showed Charlie. She found joy in their love and the love everyone else in her family had found this past year. Everyone but Abigail. Hopefully, Lucas would discover how precious Abigail was. She wanted the same for herself. Griffen offered it to her, but she allowed her fear to keep her from grasping and holding it close. Now she must deal with her fear and fight for what she most desired. She'd found the security she craved with Griffen.

"Do you mind if I stay?"

"No, we do not mind. Now if you ladies will excuse me, I have some business I must attend to." Sinclair brought Charlie's hand to his lips and placed a soft kiss on it.

Everyone in the room sighed and caused Charlie to blush. She still wasn't accustomed to the loving attention Jasper paid her in front of others. While nothing else caused her cheeks to redden, his love always did.

Charlie rolled her eyes. "Since Jasper left, you must explain why you never called off your affair with Lord Kincaid. I never had the chance to question you after Evelyn and I interrupted your game of billiards. Which, I must add, steamed the room."

Jacqueline blushed, remembering the billiards game and the bets they'd both fulfilled. "Yes, well, after a few kisses with Lord Kincaid, he tempted me into changing my mind."

"Yes, kisses from the one you most desire affects one so," Gemma gushed.

Jacqueline hesitated before making her next announcement. She only felt love and pride with the news she was about to share. And she knew none of them would judge her because they were her warm, caring family who had only ever offered support.

She took a deep breath and placed her hands across her stomach. "There is another small issue soon to grow much larger."

The reaction she received was as expected. Each lady gasped and wrapped her in a hug. Then they explained their glee, ushering Jacqueline to sit down. Charlie and Evelyn sat on each side of her, placing their hands on her stomach.

"We are going to be an aunt!" they exclaimed together.

Jacqueline laughed. "Yes. The very best of aunts."

Gemma rubbed her stomach. "We will become mamas around the same time."

Abigail smiled. "Congratulations."

Jacqueline reached out for Abigail's hand. "Do not give up hope."

Abigail wiped away a stray tear. "'Tis not about me right now, but you."

Jacqueline nodded. She understood how Abigail tired of hearing the same request. And Jacqueline couldn't blame her. It just broke her heart that they'd all found happiness while Abigail waited for Lucas to admit his feelings.

"In the meantime, what are your plans?" Charlie asked.

A devilish smile crossed Jacqueline's face. "I plan to seduce my viscount."

Chapter Twenty

Lady Forrester rushed into Colebourne's study with urgency, needing to address their current matchmaking scheme. It had escalated past a point where they must take immediate action. "Theo, we must secure Jacqueline's hand with Kincaid's immediately. You must put aside your misgivings and think of Jacqueline's future."

Colebourne set down his papers, regarding Susanna with amusement. "Calm down. I settled my differences with Kincaid this morning while we fished. Once he has cleaned up, I am allowing him a few private moments with Jacqueline. In a matter of hours, we will have achieved success with another match."

Susanna twisted her hands. "I fear we are too late. Jacqueline has fled to Charlie's, and now she is in a delicate condition."

"Fled? Why the dramatics, my dear? She pays Charlie a visit at her estate every few days."

Susanna gritted her teeth, trying to keep her patience with her brother-in-law. While she had enjoyed herself these past few months playing matchmaker with him, his schemes for this match went beyond scandalous. Now Jacqueline and Kincaid would suffer repercussions if they didn't settle this match soon.

She took a deep breath before starting her explanation. "Lord Falcone told Jacqueline about Kincaid's past. When I followed to console her, I found her emptying the contents of her stomach into a chamber pot. Then she grew tired, a condition I have witnessed recently. She takes naps often."

Colebourne waved his hand as a show of nothing of importance. "The fish upset her stomach, 'tis all. And as much as we have entertained, her tiredness is pretty excusable. As for Lord Falcone, I will admit I overstepped with my scheming. I should not have involved him in the matter. But now Kincaid's secret is out in the open for him to admit to his wrongdoings, and he can prove to Jacqueline how worthy he is of her affections."

Susanna smiled as serenely as she could before dropping her news. "She is with child, Theodore."

Colebourne's eyes widened, and he dropped back into his chair. Once the news settled in, he started laughing and clapping his enjoyment at the wonderful news. "Oh, our most excellent match to date."

Susanna shook her head, collapsing in a chair. "You are so incorrigible."

"Ah, Susanna. You must admit this couldn't be more of a perfect beginning for Jacqueline."

Susanna sighed. "Yes, I agree. She has been out of sorts without the girls seeking her advice over their troubles. Now she can have her own little one to nurture."

"And we can have another little bundle to spoil along with Gemma and Ralston's child." Theo chuckled.

"All good and well, but we must handle her disappearance to Charlie's. She packed her valise, and I don't know how long she will stay away."

Theo rubbed his hands together. "It is perfect. I will inform Kincaid of her departure and persuade him to win her over by wooing her."

Susanna raised her brows. "Are we not past the point of courting?"

"Perhaps, but the gesture will only endure Kincaid more to Jacqueline."

Susanna smirked. "Your schemes are still devious, I see."

Colebourne nodded. "And they will continue until Jacqueline weds Kincaid."

"Which will be soon, I believe. Then on to our last match."

Colebourne smiled. "Which will be our most devious match of all."

~~~~~

Kincaid nursed his glass of whiskey. As defeated as he felt, one would think he should drink himself into oblivion. But he couldn't numb his senses with the sweet nectar of alcohol. No, he must have his wits about him for whenever Jacqueline returned.

When Colebourne broke the news to him of how Jacqueline fled to her sister's house, depression had set in. However, the duke had convinced him it was only a minor setback. To gain her attention, he must woo Jacqueline with a swift courtship. Woo her? How in the hell did you woo someone you'd already seduced? Or when they'd seduced you? He wasn't sure anymore who did the seducing. And could you even woo someone who'd discovered the depth of your depravity?

Damn Falcone. Why did he have to strike out at Jacqueline with his vengeance? He'd achieved his ultimate revenge by turning her affections away from Kincaid. Was the gentleman satisfied for avenging his sister's honor now? He hadn't even gotten the chance to confront Falcone before the marquess took off for parts unknown.
~~~~~

Colebourne admitted he'd brought Falcone here to stir trouble in his matchmaking attempt. The duke loved drama and thought a little jealousy would spur Kincaid into action in securing Jacqueline's hand. Instead, it'd only sent her running. But not far enough away that he couldn't catch her.

During dinner, Lady Eden had encouraged him to stay patient. Jacqueline would return, and all would be well. It was the same advice Colebourne had offered him when assuring him Jacqueline only needed to think matters through. Patience? Any other time in his life, he could handle patience, but with Jacqueline, he feared he would lose her if he didn't act on his impatience.

Dinner had been a quiet affair. The Holbrooke ladies and Abigail Cason had remained at the Sinclair's for dinner. Evelyn and Gemma arrived back at the manor after everyone had retired to their bedchambers or moved on to other entertainments. Kincaid hadn't wanted to be alone, so he'd joined the other gentlemen in the billiard room for an evening of gambling and drinking. Except, he did neither, hence why he still held a full glass of whiskey.

Ralston strolled into the room. "Count me in on the next game."

"Shouldn't you be catering to your wife's every need?" Worth quipped.

Ralston smirked. "She is fast asleep and will not wake until dawn. So this allows me plenty of time to wipe away your fortunes."

"We shall see about that," Gray answered.

Ralston sat down next to Kincaid, stretching out his legs. He nodded to the full glass. "Troubles?"

Kincaid sighed. "More than I can count."

"Jacqueline or Colebourne?"

Kincaid scoffed. “Jacqueline. Colebourne finally offered his support.”

Ralston quirked a brow. “Very impressive. Then what troubles you?”

Before Kincaid responded, Gray answered with disgust. “Falcone spewed gossip to Jacqueline about an affair from Kincaid’s past. Then he scurried away like the coward he is.”

Kincaid shook his head. “It was not gossip but the truth of an act I committed in my youth.”

Gray growled. “Speculation. And it wasn’t his place to discuss it. Plus, we all have incidents in our past we are not proud of. Jacqueline is levelheaded and will understand.”

Kincaid remained in doubt at his friend’s encouraging words. Jacqueline may be levelheaded, but she was also a lady with high moral standards. However, she’d abandoned those standards the past three years during their torrid love affair. Would she take her actions into account while she was away? He could only hope.

“Colebourne offered his advice.”

Gray scoffed. “And what was my father’s suggestion?”

“He said I should woo her.”

All the gentlemen laughed at the absurdity of the notion.

“Woo her? You have already ruined her. This is my father’s advice?” Gray shook his head. “The man instigated Falcone into the match and caused Jacqueline to run away. Now he believes if you court her, you will win her over. He is mad, I tell you.”

“Is it madness to want your loved ones settled?” Worthington asked, joining them.

Worth groaned. "Not you, too. I hope you do not plan to follow Colebourne's lead and try to settle me into a marriage I do not want."

Worthington shook his head. "I wish for no lady alive to suffer from your attention."

The room roared with laughter at the insult. Even Worth laughed. "Any lady should hold such luck. I would make a better husband than you, my brother."

"Keep fooling yourself, Graham."

"It is madness when he interferes with everyone's lives like they are his to manipulate. Even now he schemes to bring Jacqueline back home to settle with Kincaid. Then once he accomplishes his goal, he will move on to me, and I refuse to allow him to rule my life," Gray declared.

"Settle?" Kincaid asked.

Gray cringed. "Sorry, mate. I meant to say to make a match. You and Jacqueline are perfect for one another. I meant every word when I offered my support. I only attempt to point out my father's matchmaking madness."

"No. You are trying to convince yourself your father is meddling because you keep denying your feelings for Abigail. Why fight it? You two are meant for each other," Kincaid asked.

The other gentlemen murmured their agreement.

Gray shook his head. "Because I will not subject her to the ton's ridicule. She doesn't deserve their brutal treatment. I observed how they treated her during the season, and I will not be the reason for her misery. No matter how much I care for her."

Ralston scoffed. "Since Forrester is not here, I will use his objection. Bollocks. Utter bollocks."

"I shall call him a fool," Worthington joined in.

"Coward," Kincaid replied.

"Well, since you refuse to offer for the lovely Abigail, perhaps I should," Worth baited him.

Gray advanced on Worth, pulling his arm back to land a punch, but Kincaid stepped in front of him. Gray snarled over Kincaid's shoulder. "Stay away from her," he threatened.

But Worth only quirked his eyebrow, stating he refused to listen to Gray's demand.

"Enough," Worthington demanded. "Graham, stop annoying Gray. Kincaid, you need to decide how to win over Jacqueline. You have upset my wife, and as a member of this family, I will not tolerate my sister-in-law's unhappiness."

Kincaid nodded. "I respect your stance. However, I am at a loss."

Ralston rose from his chair. "Well, then, shall we play a game of billiards and strategize your attempt to court her?"

Since there was one too many of them, Kincaid decided to sit out so he could pay attention to the advice they offered him. Each piece of advice Ralston or Worthington offered, he took to heart, but they were hopeless suggestions. It might work with their wives, but not with Jacqueline. Worth and Gray were no help since neither of them held any experience with a wife, nor did they pay court to any lady. Especially Gray, when he refused to accept the destiny laid before him. Once they had exhausted their advice, their conversation changed to another topic, leaving Kincaid to mull over his next step.

"Gemma's pregnancy wracks my nerves, between getting sick every morning and falling asleep at the drop of a hat. At least she doesn't faint anymore like she did at the start of her term. On our honeymoon, I had to catch her half a dozen times because she grew light-headed," Ralston explained.

Kincaid jerked to attention. "What are Gemma's symptoms?"

"She gets sick and sleeps all the time, and has the most extraordinary cravings. Even this morning, I made a trip into the village to get her marzipan. No matter how outrageous the request is, I will do anything to offer her comfort," Ralston explained.

Kincaid downed his drink. His hand shook as he lowered the glass and sat it down before he dropped it. Kincaid sat dumbfounded. The symptoms Jacqueline held were the same as Gemma's. Jacqueline carried their child. It explained her sickness in the middle of the night and how she fell asleep, taking frequent naps. And how the shade of her skin had changed when the smell of the fish overtook her senses. When the full thought settled, he remembered the changes in her body over the past month when they shared a bed. Her breasts were fuller and more tender. The swell of her stomach had rounded. The glow of her skin brightened, showcasing her inner beauty.

Did Jacqueline know? Of course, she must. The question was, did she plan to inform him or keep it a secret? With the power the duke yielded, she didn't have to marry. If she so chose, she could raise the child out of wedlock. Jacqueline wasn't one for London society and preferred a life in the country. So she wouldn't ever have to subject herself to the ton. No one would dare snub her without having to deal with the consequences of Colebourne's wrath. Once the child came of age, the powerful gentlemen in her family would offer their protection, too. He wouldn't even put it past Colebourne to offer a false story to cover the identity of the child's father.

All that aside, the full impact of their situation overwhelmed Kincaid. He'd compromised her, putting her in a delicate predicament, a place he never wanted for her. Kincaid wanted Jacqueline to accept his offer because she loved him, not because she felt forced to secure a child's welfare. Why hadn't he approached a courtship with her differently? She deserved so much more. The full implications of their union placed her in a shameful position. Though he held no shame from her condition. It was a miracle, a gift they would cherish for all their lives.

Every tender emotion he held for Jacqueline multiplied. She held inside her a precious being, a start to a family he had missed more than he thought since his own parents had passed years ago. They could become a family where he offered Jacqueline the security she missed. He understood her fear of losing all those she held dear. However, it was a task out of his control and left to fate.

A smile crept across his face and kept growing wider. He jumped to his feet and rushed for the door. Kincaid could no longer wait for her to return. He must declare his intentions and see where he stood.

Because he refused to abandon Jacqueline and his child.

"Where are you off to in such a rush?" Gray yelled.

"To Sinclair's place. I must see Jacqueline now." Kincaid offered no other explanation, considering he was already halfway down the hall.

Chapter Twenty-One

It wasn't until he reached the stables that he realized Gray followed him. "I thought your plan was to wait for Jacqueline's return to talk with her?"

Kincaid threw a saddle on his horse, preparing for the ride. He didn't want to wake the stable master, Emery, because of his own foolishness. "This cannot wait."

Gray asked no more questions, but readied his horse and rode out with Kincaid. He didn't understand why Kincaid couldn't wait, but he would ride along with him. His friend needed his support. Sinclair was as protective of Jacqueline as he was of Charlie. If Jacqueline didn't want to see Kincaid, then Sinclair would prevent him from seeing his cousin. And judging from Kincaid's determination, he wouldn't accept any obstacles to stand in his way. Gray hoped Jacqueline would notice Kincaid's effort and give the poor bloke a break, regardless of how she felt about Falcone's declaration. The person he'd described wasn't a reflection of who his friend was today.

Kincaid didn't know why Gray bothered to ride along, nor did he care. He played through the conversation he wanted to have with Jacqueline, trying to decide the best way to approach her pregnancy. But with each attempt, he floundered over the words and sounded like an arse. Perhaps he should seek Gray's advice. After all, he was her cousin and could offer him some wisdom on how to talk with her.

"I need your help," Kincaid muttered.

Gray smirked. "Finally, he asks."

Instead of voicing his question, he continued riding, saying nothing. How should he approach the delicate subject without angering his friend again? Gray had accepted how he'd compromised Jacqueline and offered his support for their union. The consequences of this matter would affect their entire family. Oh, well. It was best to just admit it and see where it led.

"Jacqueline carries my child. I understand how this may seem, but I need your advice on how to approach Jacqueline. You can release your anger after I talk with her. For now, please help me figure out what to say to Jacqueline," Kincaid rushed on, talking quickly so Gray couldn't interrupt.

Silence met Kincaid. Not only silence, but when he glanced over, Gray no longer rode alongside him. Kincaid stopped and turned his horse around. Gray sat a ways back with a shocked expression. Then anger crossed Gray's features before he swiftly replaced them with a smile and a nod. Kincaid didn't know what to think of Gray's reaction. Was he happy for them or did he imagine how he would beat Kincaid to a pulp? Why did he grin like a fool?

He winced. "Gray?"

"This is fantastic. Now she cannot refuse you. Let us hurry." Gray rode past him.

"Stop!" Kincaid shouted.

Gray pulled back on his reins. "Why? Is that not your reason for appearing on Sinclair's stoop in the middle of the night, other than to demand Jacqueline must marry you? It would be best if she agreed before my father learns of this news. Who knows how he might react. Though probably in your favor, as crazy as he has been lately."

Kincaid shook his head. "You do not understand. I do not want to force Jacqueline into a marriage she may not want. I only want to plead my case. What is your advice?"

Gray blew out a breath. "I understand. Sorry. I got ahead of myself. I see your dilemma. But in my opinion, you only need to tell her how much you love her and how you will protect her as your wife."

"All right. Let us continue."

Their ride continued in silence until they reached Sinclair's stable. When Gray jumped off his horse, Kincaid regarded him with speculation. "What are you about? I can handle it from here."

Gray slapped Kincaid's shoulder. "I know you can. However, I thought I would stay by your side for moral support. Or at least until I see Sinclair without his rifle."

Kincaid gulped. "Rifle?"

Gray nodded with amusement. "He is very protective of Jacqueline. They were good friends long before he married Charlie. Think of him as an overprotective brother."

"Oh." Kincaid didn't know how else to react. Where he hadn't been nervous but determined before, now he worried about Jacqueline's answer. Not to mention how he would convince Sinclair to allow him a few private moments with Jacqueline.

Kincaid turned a skeptical eye on Gray. "Why do I feel you are taking immense pleasure from my circumstances?"

Gray laughed. "How else is a friend supposed to react?"

Kincaid harrumphed. "How else."

When they reached the front entrance to Sinclair's estate, the lord himself met them on the front steps, smoking a cigar. "Well, if it is not the gentleman of the hour," he drawled.

Kincaid braced himself for a confrontation at Sinclair's sarcasm. However, Sinclair surprised him by holding out a cigar and nodded for him to take a seat. Instead, he narrowed his gaze at Gray. "While I am not surprised by Kincaid's appearance, I am concerned about why you accompanied him."

Gray puffed out his chest. "Why, for moral support. Also, I thought to run interference between the two of you if needed."

Sinclair scoffed. "Utter rubbish." He nodded over at Kincaid. "Did he fall for it?"

Gray growled. "Yes."

Sinclair laughed. "I can now understand why Colebourne finds such pleasure in this matchmaking business."

Kincaid narrowed his gaze. "I do not understand."

Sinclair nodded at Gray now. "He came with you because Abigail joined Jacqueline in staying. And as much as he denies his feelings for her, he cannot stand when she is out of his sight. He follows her around like a pup."

Gray scowled. "You are mistaken."

"No, I am not. When you can admit how much Abigail means to you, you will discover how much more pleasurable life is," Sinclair informed Gray before turning his focus on Kincaid. "How do you want to handle this? Do you want me to call her downstairs or would you like to sneak into her bedchamber?"

Kincaid's eyes widened at the offer. "You wish to help me?"

Sinclair snubbed out his cigar, rising from the steps. "Yes. I wish to put Jacqueline and you out of your misery. I know firsthand how exasperating a Holbrooke lady can be. Plus, if I can thwart Colebourne's plans and reunite you two before he can, I will find immense pleasure from seeking my revenge."

"Her bedchamber, then," Kincaid blurted out before Sinclair withdrew his offer.

Sinclair laughed. "I thought so. Follow me." He started up the steps and called over his shoulder, "You might as well come inside, Gray. We can share some spirits in my study while Kincaid attempts to win Jacqueline over. I must keep my eye on you."

"I do not need to be watched over," Gray growled.

"Oh, yes, you do. I will not have Abigail upset while in my care. Have mercy on me. I am the one who lives with Charlie now."

Kincaid laughed, and Gray muttered lowly enough they couldn't hear what he said, but it probably wasn't pleasant.

When they stepped over the threshold, Charlie was waiting impatiently, tapping her foot with her head tilted to the side, judging Kincaid as she had in the billiard room a few nights ago. "It took you long enough. For a while there, I didn't believe you would show."

"Allow me to apologize for—"

Charlie threw a bouquet of daffodils in Kincaid's arms before tugging him toward the staircase. "Here, give these to Jacqueline. They are her fav—"

"Favorite flowers," Kincaid finished.

Charlie started again. "Now she is asleep, so do not frighten her. She is a li—"

"Light sleeper."

Charlie narrowed her gaze at Kincaid's wide knowledge of her sister's sleeping habits. "She is staying in the third bedchamber once you reach the first flight of stairs. My advice is to—"

This time, Sinclair put a stop to his wife's interference. He pulled Charlie away from Kincaid and into his embrace. "Charlie, that is enough. Kincaid can take it from here." Charlie pouted at him. Sinclair placed a soft kiss on her lips. "Wish him luck."

Charlie twisted her head toward Kincaid and winked. "Good luck."

"Thank you for your help. However, it is I who underestimated you, Lady Sinclair."

Chapter Twenty-Two

He climbed the stairs and hesitated at the top. He looked down at Jacqueline's family and their encouraging support. With a nod, he continued to the third room on the left. He placed his palm on the door, working up the courage to enter the bedchamber. With a deep breath, he turned the knob and stepped inside, closing the door behind him.

He thought he would find Jacqueline asleep, but she was wide awake and sitting near the fire with a blanket wrapped around her. Waiting. Candles flickered all around her on the fireplace mantle, casting her in a warm glow. She had scattered pillows and blankets on the floor. When he turned his gaze on her, she smiled seductively and then lowered her lashes coyly before raising them again. Had the minx set out to seduce him? The scene reminded him of the first time they'd made love.

They had shared a kiss in the secret passageway, and she'd led him to her bedchamber. A quilt and an array of pillows had sat near the fireplace, offering them comfort when they explored the depths of their desires. Why had he not realized it before? She had seduced him clear back then. And here he had convinced himself he was an unscrupulous gentleman.

As he gazed upon her, he thought of how delightful a creature she was. Her caring nature, her patience, her love for all that she held dear, and how she made him feel like he could conquer the world. She was wrapped up in one amazing lady. And he knew she was his by her smile. However, he wanted to humble himself before her and seek redemption.

Griffen strode to her and handed her the flowers. "These are for you."

Jacqueline brought them to her face and breathed in their heavenly scent. "My favorite. You remembered." She knew her sister had gathered them in the garden before Griffen arrived. She had watched Charlie from the window, wondering what she was about. Her act proved her acceptance of Griffen for a brother-in-law.

Griffen appeared offended. "Of course. I remember everything about you. But I must admit, it was Charlie who picked them."

He waited for Jacqueline's response, but she only sat smiling at him and rubbing the petals between her fingers. He remained at a loss on how to proceed. Perhaps he shouldn't have let Sinclair stop Charlie from giving him instructions. He could use them now. He paced away from her, running his hand through his hair.

Jacqueline should put Griffen out of his misery. It was cruel to stay silent. But she enjoyed watching him unravel with uncertainty. Any other time, Griffen commanded a room with his standoffish character. Sometimes never showing amusement of any kind, always serious. Except she'd seen another side of his personality he didn't reveal to many people. While the ton thought him a serious lord who abided by the correct decorum, he was a lord full of contradictions to her. His visit since the wedding proved how erratic he had become. All because of her. He was perfect for her. What wasn't there to love about Griffen?

"All right, here it is. I am just going to state my intentions. I am clueless about how to proceed. If I sound demanding and state what will happen, I risk scaring you away. If I threaten to go to your uncle, you will refuse my suit and never speak to me again. However, if I plead with you, my damn pride will suffer. Yet, I will suffer through anything for your love. My greatest wish is for us to decide together. But I fear it is too late for that."

Kincaid was a coward for not facing Jacqueline. Instead, he spoke to the window, staring out into the darkness. When she remained silent, he closed his eyes in defeat. He had hoped from the scene she'd set that he still held a chance. But he was mistaken.

The soft caress of her fingertips fluttered along his back. Each touch made him aware of her nearness. Her hands slid around and peeled off his suit coat. Once it dropped to the floor, she tugged his shirt out of his trousers. Her hands snuck underneath and raked across his back.

He drew in a breath at the heat scorching him. "Jacqueline, we must—"

She pressed her lips to the middle of his back, the soft gesture seeping through the fabric. "Shh. Has anyone ever informed you how you talk too much, Lord Kincaid? Especially when a lady is trying to seduce you. It is most rude."

He swiftly turned around, catching her unaware, and swept her up into his arms. He strode across the room and laid her on the makeshift bed on the floor before she uttered another quip, lowering himself next to her. "Please forgive me, Lady Jacqueline. My manners were most atrocious." He laid on his back with his hands behind his head. "Please continue with your seduction."

The minx crawled over him and discarded the blanket, shocking him with her scanty attire. "Jacqueline," he croaked out.

Jacqueline set about unbuttoning his shirt, an innocent expression lighting her face. "Yes, Griffen?"

"Where…?" He couldn't finish his thought, struck speechless by how her breasts spilled out of the sheer negligee.

The bold sapphire caressed her curves, molding itself to every dip. A long slit on each side gave her the ability to straddle him and press herself against his hardening cock. Each time she shifted, he groaned at the sensation she stirred in him. He lifted his hands to run along the soft silk, but she grasped his wrists and lowered them back to the floor.

Her tongue clicked against the roof of her mouth. "Tsk, tsk. How can I seduce you if you cannot keep your hands to yourself?"

He chuckled. "How do you expect me to lie still underneath you when you are a tempting package I wish to unwrap?"

Jacqueline lowered and whispered in his ear, "I have no wish for you to. Unwrap me, my lord."

Kincaid pushed her hair back and cupped her cheeks. "I plan to. But we must talk."

"I only wish to love you."

He drew her closer, their lips but a breath apart. "As long as I can love you in return."

"Forever." Jacqueline sighed before sinking her mouth onto his.

When their lips met, a shift of the unknown settled them into each other's arms. Their kiss melded together, clinging to capture every sigh and whisper of their love for one another.

It took little to seduce Griffen. At the first touch of her lips upon his, he was powerless to stop himself from loving her. He helped her discard his clothing and swept the negligee off her. In between soft, slow kisses and gentle caresses, they loved one another.

Not wanting to press her to the hard floor while he made love to her, he guided Jacqueline back over him. Not only did he wish to protect her and the babe, but he wanted Jacqueline to understand the power he gave her by letting her have control. He never wanted to dominate or control her actions. He only wished to remain in her life, any way she would have him.

Jacqueline gazed into Griffen's eyes. The love shining from them used to overwhelm her. Now she welcomed the powerful emotion. She hoped he could read the same in her gaze. If not, she would express her love every day they were fortunate to spend with one another.

Jacqueline rose on her knees and trailed her hand along his chest, wrapping her hand around his cock and sliding him inside her. Slowly lowering until Griffen filled her soul, she wrapped around him and rotated her hips, drawing out his groans one after another.

Griffen felt like he had died and gone to heaven at the exquisite thrill coursing through him. Each rise of her hips built his need higher, only to rush down when she lowered herself. And each time before he crashed, she would tighten around him, vibrating with her own pleasure.

The goddess had been created to love him. Her hair cascaded down her back, and her lips were plump from the kisses they shared. A glow shimmered off her body, enveloping him in her happiness.

He drew her hands into his and guided them to rest against his heart. "I love you, Jacqueline."

Those simple words filled Jacqueline's soul with peace. She no longer feared the love he gifted her with. Instead, she cherished them.

She moved their hands to cover her heart. "I love you, Griffen."

Then she lowered her head and kissed him with every ounce of love she held for him. He pulled her head closer, devouring her lips. He hungered for the taste of her and stroked their tongues against each other. The kisses built their passion higher, demanding to find solace.

He grabbed her hips and surged upwards. Jacqueline gripped his arms, and when he rose, she drew her hips downward. Each time they met, the friction increased, leaving them more desperate to reach the ecstasy they found with one another.

Jacqueline found herself unraveling further out of control. With each slide of Griffen's cock inside her, she wanted to weep at the beauty of their lovemaking. She clung to Griffen as he sent them soaring into the clouds. As always, he caught her in his embrace, and they drifted into the cocoon made for them.

Before she could nestle against him, Griffen rose with her in his arms and carried her to the bed. He drew a blanket over them and placed a hand over her stomach. Jacqueline gave him a puzzled look. "I wish to make the mother of my child more comfortable."

Jacqueline gasped. "You know?"

"Aye."

Jacqueline covered his hand with hers. "How?"

He intertwined their fingers together. "Ralston described Gemma's condition, and you shared similar ailments. It drew me to conclude that our time together resulted in this miracle."

Jacqueline started crying. "You think it is a miracle?"

"Aye. Is it not?" He swiped away a tear.

"Yes."

Griffen sighed. "Ahh, love. I have given you more doubt about accepting my hand in marriage. If you will allow me the chance to explain myself."

Jacqueline turned on her side and gave him a gentle kiss. "There is no need to explain yourself. I love you for who you are and do not judge you for your past actions. But if you want to tell me, I will listen. Although, to be honest, I do not believe a word Lord Falcone spoke."

The truth weighed on him, but his guilt pushed him to tell her the truth. He wasn't the innocent party in the scandal. It was his pursuit of the duchess that had led to the downfall of his character. Only with Colebourne's interference was he able to avoid further destruction of his name.

"Every word Falcone told you was true. Or his perception of the truth. A few years ago, I became quite enamored with the Duchess of Gostwicke. From what I understood, her father had arranged her marriage to the duke. The duke was aloof with his new bride, and I thought to console her. My pursuit angered Gostwicke. I am ashamed of myself and my actions during this incident. However, at the time, I refused to accept her rejections and wanted to best the duke."

He paused for a minute before continuing. "After indulging a few cups at the club, I goaded Gostwicke into accepting a bet. Whoever won the game of billiards won the affections of the duchess. We were down to the final shot, and luckily for both of our sakes, we didn't draw a crowd. But Colebourne happened upon our game and intercepted. I don't remember how, but he convinced Gostwicke to halt the game and not to pursue vengeance against me. Colebourne dragged me out of the club and dropped me off at my townhome. When I awoke in the morning, he sat waiting for me. It was then I promised years of servitude to him. Which led me to attend to his every request. However, I don't regret any of it. Because it led me to you."

"Not even your affection for the duchess?" There was a hint of jealousy in Jacqueline's tone.

He tried to hide his smile but failed. "Not even for her."

Jacqueline's lips pinched with her displeasure. "Is that so?"

Griffen laughed. "Yes, because without my dalliance with the duchess, I would have never understood the difference between a simple infatuation and the love I hold for you. Try as I might, I cannot undo my past. I can only learn from my mistakes and move forward. Do you need more explanation on my past?"

Jacqueline thought it over and understood it for what it was. A mistake in his youth. From his mistake, he had learned a lesson, one he showed with his every action since then. "No, there is no need to explain yourself further. We shall leave this topic in the past where it belongs."

"Now that we have cleared that matter, why did you run?"

Jacqueline sighed. "It was foolish, considering I eagerly welcomed you in my bed after you chased after me."

Griffen kissed her shoulder. "That you did, my lady." His lips trailed lowered.

She wiggled around, drawing his attention back to her, not her breasts. "Focus, Lord Kincaid."

Griffen gifted her with a charming smile before drawing her across his chest. "Yes, my lady. Do proceed with your explanation."

She folded her hands under her chin. "I suppose I allowed Lord Falcone's slander to give me another excuse to deny our love. But once I arrived here, I realized my mistake. Then I grew furious at how he'd degraded your name without giving you a chance to defend yourself. And I did the same. Instead of standing by you, I fell into his plans to ruin our bond. And for that, I apologize to you."

Griffen nodded, accepting her apology. "And the babe?"

An angelic smile spread across her face. "I only recently realized myself."

"How far along are you?"

"At least two months, if not more. Either from our time in London or when you first arrived for Lucas's wedding."

Kincaid turned serious. "You know of my desire for you to become my bride. Now more so than ever. But I don't want you to assume my offer is because you are with child, especially since I've asked before. I want to marry you, Jacqueline, because I love you. The child is only an extra blessing. But if you decide you do not wish to wed me, I will try to accept your terms. I only ask for your patience if I cannot understand."

Jacqueline slid her hand over his cheek. "I will marry you, my love. After I fled, I realized how I'd run away from my other half. You have become a part of me that I never want to lose. I allowed my fear of the loss of my parents to keep us apart. I never wanted to grow close to anyone because I feared their loss if they would perish. Life comes with no guarantees, and one cannot live in fear of the unexpected. If so, then they never truly live. I needed to learn this, and now I have. So, my love, I accept your love and proposal. Now we only need to convince Uncle Theo of your honorable intentions."

He tapped her on the nose. "No need. Your uncle and I had a long discussion while we were fishing and we have settled our differences. If you wouldn't have fled, you would have learned how he has given us his blessing."

Jacqueline blushed at her mishap. "He has?"

"Yes."

"Did he change his mind on your business venture? I know how eager you were to get his acceptance. It is a fine idea that I am most proud of you for. Would you like me to talk to him for you?"

"No. Although, I thank you for the offer. We also discussed it while fishing and agreed it was not a venture he could help me with."

Jacqueline frowned, disappointed in her uncle. "Do not worry, I will help you think of an alternative route to make your plan a success."

Griffen squeezed her in a hug. "Ahh, it warms my heart how devoted you are to my cause. But do not fret, my love. I have acquired two business partners."

Jacqueline's brows drew together. "Who?"

"Graham Worthington and Ralston. We decided it will merge well with their business. We will keep it separate, and once it is on solid ground, Ralston will offer me the option to buy back his initial investment."

"This is wonderful news."

Griffen stared in Jacquelin's eyes and spoke from the heart. "I realize I have nothing to offer you in the way of financial stability. I cannot provide you with the grand lifestyle your sisters and cousin live in. All that I can offer you is my love and utter devotion. I will cherish you and our children every day of my life."

Jacqueline pushed Griffen's hair back. "Oh, love, I am sorry I gave you doubt about the love I hold for you. None of that matters. I only wish for a simple life. You know I am not one for grand affairs. I shall find contentment in whatever fashion we live in as long as you are nearby."

Kincaid leaned into her palm. "Never once will I leave your side. I know you wish to live in the country, but while I start my business, we must stay in London. Once I have the correct men in place, we can retire to our estate, where I'm afraid we must work to make repairs. Sadly, I have let the house fall to neglect."

Jacqueline fought back a yawn. "One we can repair together."

Kincaid frowned. "A discussion for another time. For now, you need your rest."

Jacqueline clasped his arms, holding him still. "Please do not leave."

He eased her grip. "I have no intention of leaving your side ever again, my love."

She relaxed and settled her head on his shoulder. "Excellent," she murmured before falling asleep.

Kincaid chuckled and settled the covers tighter around him. By all rights, he should rise and leave her bed before any of Sinclair's servants discovered him. Not only the servants but Sinclair himself. But he meant what he'd told Jacqueline, and he was a gentleman who stood by his word. Gray would have to return on his own or wait until morning to escort the ladies home. His eyes drifted shut, and he soon joined Jacqueline in sleep.

Chapter Twenty-Three

Gray spent an uncomfortable night sleeping on a parlor chair. He waited for Sinclair and Charlie to join him, but they had snuck away, leaving him alone with his bloody thoughts. He kept fighting the urge to find Abigail. She slept in a bedchamber upstairs, but he didn't know which one. He cared about her too deeply to rouse rumors of her virtue.

An innocent virtue was all a lady had to keep her standing in society. As a miss born into low beginnings, Abigail suffered from the stigma of not holding the title of a lady. While his family felt differently toward Abigail, some held the lowest opinion they could. They spent their life not appreciating the fortune of wealth they were born into.

He stretched and twisted his neck back and forth to ease the aching muscles. He should have awakened a servant and requested a bed, but he'd thought they would return to Colebourne Manor after Kincaid settled the matter with Jacqueline. However, the scoundrel kept ruining his cousin, and now the servants were soon to rise and start their daily chores. He needed to get Kincaid downstairs before any rumors started. Even though Kincaid and Jacqueline would soon wed, once the babe was born and every matron of the ton counted the dates on their fingers, speculation would surround them.

So as not to draw notice, Gray put himself to right and climbed the stairs. There were two closed doors. Now, which one was Jacqueline's bedchamber? He pressed his ear to the first door. A soft hum whispered through the panel, then angelic lyrics swept through him. Gray closed his eyes once he realized it was Abigail. He pressed his hands against the door as if he were reaching out to her, only to draw them away with reluctance and step back. He fought his inner desires and stalked over to the other door.

He refused to delve into his reaction to Abigail so nearby. If he did, he couldn't hold himself back from flinging the door open, taking her into his arms, and ravishing her like he did every night in his dreams. He craved a kiss from her sweet mouth. However, one kiss would never satisfy the intense need he held for Abigail. He must grab Kincaid and get the hell out of Sinclair's home. The sooner, the better for his peace of mind.

He rapped his knuckles against the door. "Kincaid," he hissed.

When nobody answered, he tried the knob, but it wouldn't budge. He pounded harder. He'd lost what patience he clung to. Gray should have stopped Kincaid from traveling here.

"Leave them alone," a soft voice whispered behind him.

Gray stilled. Her flowery scent washed over him, and the sound of her voice sent shivers racing along his spine. The very lady he fancied and fought to keep his emotions in check with stood so close by. All he had to do was turn and he could capture her in his arms, bend his head, and brush his lips across hers. Would Abigail sigh into their kiss? Would she taste like the candy she secretly savored when she thought nobody watched her?

Before he could react to his desires, he heard her footsteps walking away. He swung around and saw her skirts round the corner. He glanced at the door and back toward Abigail. "Ah, hell."

Gray strode after Abigail as his thoughts of protecting Jacqueline from rumors fled with his one chance to spend time alone with Abigail. She had avoided him since Duncan and Selina's wedding. Every time he sought her company, someone acted as a buffer to keep him from her.

"Abigail." He tried to get her to stop, but she continued down the stairs. "Abigail." Gray's voice raised, but that only made her walk faster. However, her smaller steps were no match for his long strides. He passed her and stepped in front of her, blocking her path.

Abigail pinched her lips. "Please, step aside, Lord Gray."

Gray growled. "Must you keep up with your insistence on addressing me with such formality? At one time I was Lucas, and you were Abigail."

"Those occurrences are in the past. If I am to secure the role of a governess, I must learn to properly address my betters. And you, Lord Gray, are my better. A fact you made clear at the start of the season." She stepped around him and proceeded to the breakfast room.

Gray swung around and followed her. "Will you ever allow us to pass from that awkward conversation? You misconstrued what I meant."

Abigail smiled at Charlie and Sinclair before sitting down. "No, you were quite clear, my lord."

"What was Lucas clear on?" Charlie asked.

"Nothing!"

After Gray snarled, Abigail explained. "The matter of how I should not have entered the season's entertainments because of my societal standings."

Charlie's gaze widened. "Is that why you decided to attend the functions?"

Abigail nodded before stirring sugar in the tea the servant poured for her. She blew on the warm brew and took a sip.

"That was bloody preposterous of you, Gray. Why would you insult our dear Abigail in that manner?" Sinclair asked. "I know quite a few gentlemen who are eager to court Abby. She only needs to give her permission and a line of suitors will be at her feet."

Abigail blushed. "Thank you, Jasper. But I am eager to start the next journey of my life on my own accord."

Charlie reached across the table and gripped Abigail's hand. "You have our support but know that Jasper's offer is always standing."

Gray pointed at Sinclair. "You address me as Lord Gray, yet you address him as Jasper?"

Abigail smirked. "He is a close friend."

"And I am what?"

"A lord of the ton who I must respect his rank and not overstep it by becoming too familiar."

Sinclair rose and rounded the table. It was best to remove Gray before the bloke offended Abigail again. Gray had the tendency to speak without thinking his thoughts through rationally when his emotions got the better of him. Much like Charlie. "Let us see to having a carriage readied to escort the ladies home. You and Kincaid need to arrive separately so as not to bring attention toward the ladies."

"Too late for that," Gray muttered, following Sinclair from the room. He glanced over his shoulder to find Charlie smirking her amusement at him and Abigail ignoring him as if he had never even been there.

"Perhaps so. But I am sure Colebourne already has a plan to smooth it over."

"As always, my father's madness will prevail."

Sinclair chuckled. "That it will. However, your madness toward Abigail is beyond control."

"I only wish she would see reason and know her position."

Sinclair stopped and confronted Gray. "And what do you deem her position to be?"

"Why, as a member of our family. Not as a servant to another family. Why would she sacrifice the comforts my father has provided her with to place herself in what could be an unpleasant position?"

"Perhaps because she feels she does not belong and wishes to discover a home where she might. Her friends are starting their own families, and she longs for the same."

Gray scoffed. "She belongs at Colebourne Manor."

Sinclair shook his head at Gray's foolishness. Gray didn't understand, and it would take a miracle for him to. Colebourne would handle it, but the duke would need the entire family's help to make happen. "I hold the same opinion, but voicing your foolish demands will not convince Abigail otherwise." And since Gray wouldn't admit to how he felt about Abigail, it didn't make his case any easier.

Gray frowned. "My demands are not foolish."

Sinclair slapped him on the back. "However you need to convince yourself, my friend."

"What is Lucas trying to convince himself of?" Jacqueline asked.

They turned to find Jacqueline and Kincaid standing on the bottom step, holding hands. Both of them wore a smile full of happiness. Gray snarled at them, knowing they would agree with Sinclair. Before answering them, he stalked off to the stables.

"Gray is making demands of Abigail again in her new position and how she needs to remain at Colebourne Manor. I told him he was foolish, and he refuses to admit to his mistakes on how he treats Abigail," Sinclair explained.

"It will be no small feat for Uncle Theo to make their match." Jacqueline said.

"No, it shall not. Am I the first to offer my congratulations?"

Kincaid lifted their joined hands and kissed Jacqueline's fingers. "You are."

"Excellent. I am off to ready a carriage to drive the ladies home."

After Sinclair left, Kincaid stepped down, swinging Jacqueline off the steps and around in a circle. Her laughter bounced off the walls. "I'd best ride ahead and make myself presentable before we speak to your uncle."

"I shall miss you." Jacqueline's smile beamed up at him.

Kincaid bent his head and took her lips beneath his, kissing her slowly. He drew out their affection until he heard a soft harrumph behind them. He reluctantly pulled away, but not before pressing his lips against hers for one more. "And I you, my love." He looked behind them to see Charlie and Abigail grinning their amusement at them. "Good morning, ladies."

Charlie smirked. "Good morning, Lord Kincaid. Did you sleep well?"

Kincaid smiled at Jacqueline. "Yes, my lady. Thank you for your hospitality."

"'Tis nothing. However, I think it wise for you to take your leave before the servants gossip."

Kincaid nodded. "Yes, I agree." He lifted Jacqueline's hand to his lips and pressed a kiss across her knuckles. "I will await your return with eagerness."

Jacqueline sighed as Kincaid walked away. His renewed confidence showed in his swagger. As much as she enjoyed him walking toward her, him walking away from her was a sight upon itself.

Charlie and Abigail sighed behind her. "Yes, I made an excellent match, if I do not say so myself," Charlie quipped.

Jacqueline laughed, hugging her sister. "I do not think Uncle Theo will give you the credit."

Charlie winked. "We shall see about that."

Abigail hooked her arms in her friends', and they started toward the front of the house, where Sinclair had instructed the carriage to wait. "I will have to agree with Jacqueline. While Uncle Theo may need help with his matchmaking at times, he will not allow another to take credit."

Charlie continued to argue her case as they climbed into the carriage. Sinclair smiled fondly at his wife as he waited outside the carriage for the ladies to enter. During the entire ride to Colebourne Manor, she didn't let up on her argument, even when the other ladies laughed at her points. Because in the end, it didn't matter who claimed victory. Only the success of another match mattered, one that included a bonus with the union. Uncle Theo would declare this the grandest match yet. Not only did he wish to see his wards married off, but he also hoped for little ones to follow.

Chapter Twenty-Four

Jacqueline tentatively knocked on the door to her uncle's study. She attempted a smile at Griffen, who smiled back at her in encouragement. When her uncle bade them to enter, they walked in holding hands to find Uncle Theo sitting in his favorite chair and Aunt Susanna sitting across from him. They were discussing the seating arrangements for dinner that evening. Their smiles welcomed Jacqueline and Kincaid closer. Uncle Theo's smile held a smidge of victory to it, and his eyes twinkled with his enjoyment.

"I told you, my love. He wholeheartedly approves," Kincaid whispered in her ear.

"He really does," she answered in awe.

"Come in, children, and take a seat." Colebourne waved them toward the sofa.

Aunt Susanna peered at them before looking at Colebourne. "Yes, a mighty fine couple they make. I told you he was the perfect gentleman for Jacqueline."

Colebourne nodded. "That you did, Susanna. You always had perfect taste."

"Still do."

Colebourne roared with laughter. "Yes, I misspoke. Sorry, my dear."

Susanna chuckled. "I forgive you."

Jacqueline sighed, shaking her head at their theatrics. "We are sitting right here. I hate to discredit both of you, but Griffen and I made our own match years before you started this matchmaking madness."

Colebourne raised his brow. "Is that so?"

Kincaid gulped at the duke's glare. Perhaps Jacqueline had the right of growing nervous at admitting to their affair. "Yes."

Jacqueline squeezed Kincaid's hand. "There is no need for an explanation, nor will we offer one. We wish to share with you my acceptance of Lord Kincaid's offer to become his wife."

Colebourne frowned. "And if I withdraw my support?"

Jacqueline shrugged. "Then we shall leave this evening for Scotland. But I do not think you will. I, for one, have it on great authority that you already knew of my affair with Kincaid and encouraged it. Also, you pretended displeasure with him, only to further entice him in my eyes. I am onto your devious schemes, Uncle Theo. I have been from the start."

Colebourne's smile grew shrewd. "Ah, you think you have me figured out, do you, missy?"

Jacqueline laughed. "Yes, I do."

"Who gave me away?" Colebourne narrowed his gaze on Susanna.

Susanna gave Colebourne a charming smile. "I needed to take matters into my own hands when you brought Lord Falcone into the scheme. A mistake on your part, one I disagreed with."

Colebourne sighed. "Yes, a blunder we thankfully recovered from by the sight before me. I apologize, Kincaid."

Kincaid nodded his forgiveness. He knew Colebourne had acted in desperation when he invited Lord Falcone to the estate. It was in the past, a place he wanted to keep his own blunders. His future sharing a family with Jacqueline was all that mattered.

"May I ask if you still hold on to the fear of losing those you love?" Aunt Susanna asked.

Jacqueline chose her words carefully. "That fear will always remain with me, but with Griffen's love, I can overcome the struggle and cherish our time together. Some days it might try to break through, but Griffen will help me fight the demons before they take hold."

"That I will, my love." He pressed a kiss to her head.

Colebourne clapped his hands together with enthusiasm. "And the babe?"

Jacqueline's eyes widened. "You know?"

"Aye," Colebourne and Susanna answered at once.

"And you are not ashamed?"

"Ashamed?" Colebourne muttered. "No, my girl, I am proud beyond words can say. Now I can have another babe to bounce on my knee along with Gemma and Ralston's babe. Wish those others would hurry. I am not getting any younger."

Tears streamed down Jacqueline's cheeks at her uncle's caring support. "I do not know what to say. I feared I'd brought shame upon our family."

Colebourne stood up and beckoned for her to come closer. "Ahh, Jacqueline. You can never bring shame to our family. You kept us from sinking into a hole we could never climb out of. With your guidance and love through the years, those girls flourished into amazing ladies. With your support and love, you helped an old man and his son grieve and learn to live without a part of their soul. I find such joy in the love you found with Kincaid and you will make a wonderful mother."

Aunt Susanna came over to them, wiped away her tears, and pulled Jacqueline into her arms. "You are the strength of our family and will remain so. Allow no one to find satisfaction in judging you because you are above them, and their opinion matters not. They are nothing but a bunch of old English biddies."

Jacqueline laughed through her tears at their simple acceptance. "I love both of you."

"And we love you." Colebourne beamed and held out his hand to Kincaid. "Welcome to the family, Kincaid."

Kincaid shook Colebourne's hand and accepted Lady Forrester's hug. Everyone settled back into their seats, and they discussed the small wedding Jacqueline wanted. Colebourne agreed and sent notice to have the banns read. Colebourne asked for a simple request in return. He wished for them to travel to Susanna and Ramsay's estate to celebrate Christmas. He explained how the other couples had agreed, and it would warm his heart if they did, too. Colebourne wanted to end the year with his family before they each went their separate ways. They agreed to his wish. Jacqueline could never refuse her uncle, and Kincaid would forever owe the duke a debt of gratitude.

Jacqueline and Kincaid rose to leave. "And Abigail and Lucas?"

"Do not fret, my dear. Susanna and I have plans." He winked at Susanna.

Susanna smiled mischievously. "That we do."

Jacqueline looked to heaven. "Ah, the madness continues."

Epilogue

"Perhaps we should stay on for a couple of extra days until you feel better," Griffen tried to persuade Jacqueline.

They had been traveling the past few days on their way to spend Christmas at the Forrester's estate in Scotland. As the day drew to an end, the traveling party settled at an inn along the route. While the rest of the family settled belowstairs in a private room to eat dinner, Griffen and Jacqueline declined, pleading exhaustion. The innkeeper delivered them a meal they enjoyed while stretched out across the bed.

She opened her eyes to his weary expression. While she wanted to continue on with the rest of her family, her husband's offer sounded most welcoming. She still suffered from nausea at first light, and the pace they traveled made for an uncomfortable ride. The carriage held the luxuries for the rough travel, but her body protested each time they hit a rut in the road, which only added to Griffen's worries. At this moment, she would agree to anything to help settle his fussy behavior toward her.

"I agree," she complied.

Griffen didn't wait for her to say another word before he left their room at the inn. He didn't stay away long and came back looking lighter on his feet and wearing a satisfactory grin. "Your uncle agrees, too. Ralston and Gemma reached the same conclusion and will also remain behind. We can ride in their carriage instead of finding a lesser mode of transportation to convey in."

Jacqueline sighed. "Wonderful."

Relief settled over Griffen at Jacqueline's compliance. He refused to be one of those husbands who made demands and expected his wife to follow whether or not she approved. But he would have if she didn't agree on this matter. The farther they traveled, the more distress she grew, not wanting to admit how fragile her continuance was because of her pregnancy. Thankfully, she finally showed her family her vulnerability, instead of pretending all was well.

He bent to give her a kiss and noticed she was fast asleep, a regular occurrence during the past month. He chuckled. While most gentlemen wouldn't enjoy a marriage of this type, he found it most fulfilling. He wouldn't trade any part of it. Jacqueline was a dream come true, and he was one lucky bastard. He discarded his clothing and slid underneath the covers, pulling Jacqueline into his arms.

Jacqueline awoke and snuggled closer to the warmth. She yawned and stretched, her body wiggling against her husband.

"Keep still, wench. Your husband is trying to sleep."

"Wench? Is that any way to address the mother of your child?" Jacqueline tugged on his hair.

Griffen rolled them over, hovering above her. He was careful to keep his weight from causing her any harm. "It is when she lies naked in my arms, tempting me to have scandalous thoughts."

A seductive smile graced her mouth. "What kind of scandalous thoughts?"

He nipped her shoulder before trailing his lips to her breasts, where he paused and blew out a soft breath. Her nipples hardened, and he stuck his tongue out to lavish them. Her moan declared her approval. "The kind where I ravish your body while you scream my name with your pleasure."

Jacqueline guided his head to her other breast. "Perhaps you should act upon them, so I have a better understanding. I need more of a demonstration to fully appreciate how your mind works."

"Something like this?" Griffen asked, sliding his fingers into her wetness, coating them with its warmth.

Jacqueline arched her body. "Yes, but perhaps you might use this instead." She stroked her hand along his cock, wrapping her fingers around him.

He captured her hands and brought them above her head. His restraint was near to bursting. "Wench, you almost unmanned me," he growled.

"Mmm," she murmured, licking her lips.

Griffen dropped her hands and ran them through her hair, bringing her lips to his for a kiss so unforgettable they would remember it to their last dying breaths. He didn't stop there but spent the evening into the next morning worshipping Jacqueline as the tempting wench she was. Each time they made love, their bond grew stronger, intertwining their souls into one. And each day he showed Jacqueline how much he cherished her, never leaving her in doubt of their love.

Jacqueline saw the sunrise in Griffen's arms, his fingers tangled in her hair. When they stilled and his breathing grew heavy, she rolled over and propped her hands on his chest, watching him sleep. She was the luckiest lady on earth to land the proper Lord Kincaid. Only she knew how improper he was.

Her fingers feathered through his hair. To think she'd almost let her fear of losing someone she loved to keep her from embracing his love. But to his never-ending pursuit, she realized how dreadful her life would be without his love. And she'd learned to welcome the uncertainty and embrace it with open arms.

After all, love was a madness everyone should succumb to.

Look for Lucas & Abigail's story in January/February 2022!

If you would like to hear my latest news then visit my website www.lauraabarnes.com to join my mailing list.

"Thank you for reading How the Lady Seduced the Viscount. Gaining exposure as an independent author relies mostly on word-of-mouth, so if you have the time and inclination, please consider leaving a short review wherever you can."

Author Laura A. Barnes

International selling author Laura A. Barnes fell in love with writing in the second grade. After her first creative writing assignment, she knew what she wanted to become. Many years went by with Laura filling her head full of story ideas and some funny fish songs she wrote while fishing with her family. Thirty-seven years later, she made her dreams a reality. With her debut novel *Rescued By the Captain*, she has set out on the path she always dreamed about.

When not writing, Laura can be found devouring her favorite romance books. Laura is married to her own Prince Charming (who for some reason or another thinks the heroes in her books are about him) and they have three wonderful children and two sweet grandbabies. Besides her love of reading and writing, Laura loves to travel. With her passport stamped in England, Scotland, and Ireland; she hopes to add more countries to her list soon.

While Laura isn't very good on the social media front, she loves to hear from her readers. You can find her on the following platforms:

You can visit her at ***www.lauraabarnes.com*** to join her mailing list.

Website: **http://www.lauraabarnes.com**

Amazon: **https://amazon.com/author/lauraabarnes**

Goodreads: **https://www.goodreads.com/author/show/16332844.Laura_A_Barnes**

Facebook: **https://www.facebook.com/AuthorLauraA.Barnes/**

Instagram: **https://www.instagram.com/labarnesauthor/**

Twitter: **https://twitter.com/labarnesauthor**

BookBub: **https://www.bookbub.com/profile/laura-a-barnes**

Desire more books to read by Laura A. Barnes

Enjoy these other historical romances:

<u>Matchmaking Madness Series:</u>

How the Lady Charmed the Marquess

How the Earl Fell for His Countess

How the Rake Tempted the Lady

How the Scot Stole the Bride

How the Lady Seduced the Viscount

<u>Tricking the Scoundrels Series:</u>

Whom Shall I Kiss... An Earl, A Marquess, or A Duke?

Whom Shall I Marry... An Earl or A Duke?

I Shall Love the Earl

The Scoundrel's Wager

The Forgiven Scoundrel

<u>Romancing the Spies Series:</u>

Rescued By the Captain

Rescued By the Spy

Rescued By the Scot

Printed in Great Britain
by Amazon

74820643R00135